# daring
the **bad** boy

an Endless Summer novel

# MONICA MURPHY

Entangled Publishing, LLC
2614 South Timberline Road
Suite 109
Fort Collins, CO 80525
Visit our website at www.entangledpublishing.com.

Crush is an imprint of Entangled Publishing, LLC.

Edited by Stacy Abrams
Cover design by Bree Archer
Cover art from iStock

Manufactured in the United States of America

First Edition August 2016

*This story is dedicated to my daughter Amy and her friends, who help keep me young. Who also keep me updated on the latest trends, who introduce me to songs I probably would've never heard of (hello, "Right Hand" by Drake—thanks, Bobbee), and who are all a genuine joy to spend time with. This book is for every one of you—love you girls!*

# Chapter One

ANNIE

"Don't forget to pack extras of everything," Mom stressed, her voice high, her entire demeanor anxious. She really didn't want me to leave, though she was the one who'd suggested I go to camp in the first place. And I guess I can't blame her, since I am her only child, but it's just for a few weeks—I had to be wait-listed, and when a spot opened up for the second session, I begged my parents to let me go.

But with the way she's fretting over my leaving, I realize she needs to cut the umbilical cord sometime. At least I'll be outside getting fresh air, not stuck in the air-conditioned house with my nose in a book. That's how I usually spend my summers.

Well, no more.

Not that there's anything wrong with reading, but…it was my escape, my safe place. I'm tired of living in someone else's imaginary world—I want to live in *my* world for once. But it's hard making a new impression on people you've known your entire school life, some of them since preschool.

To them I'm quiet little Annie McFarland. The girl who cried so hard on the first day of kindergarten that she blew a bubble of snot out her nose. The girl who was so petrified to perform in the third-grade Christmas play that her knees literally knocked together and everyone could hear them. The girl who had a major crush on Wade Johnson in sixth grade and wrote him a heartfelt Valentine's Day poem—and he shared it with all his friends.

I endured their teasing for the rest of the school year. Sixth grade was definitely not my favorite year.

Yeah. I could go on and on.

I'd just finished my sophomore year, and while everyone was busy pairing off, being social, actually doing something with their lives, I was stuck. Stuck in my quiet shell, stuck with the nerd-girl label, stuck as the teacher's pet. I hated it.

More than anything, I was beyond ready for a change.

"Extra T-shirts, extra shorts." Mom ticked off the items with her fingers, her gaze meeting mine. "Extra, um, feminine products."

My cheeks went hot. "I've already packed extra everything." I waved a hand at my open but mostly stuffed duffel bag.

"Okay, good. Good. Wouldn't want you to run out of necessities. Though I fully plan on sending you care packages. And there's parents' weekend, too, so I can always bring you whatever you might need." Mom was rambling. A sure sign she was upset.

"Mom." I went to her and took her hand, giving it a squeeze. "I don't leave for another twenty-four hours. It's not time to cry yet."

"I'll just miss you." She brushed a stray hair away from my forehead, her gaze soft. "You've never left us like this before, for this long. A whole month, hundreds of miles away.

With *strangers.*" She stressed the last word.

That was my favorite part of the plan. Being with strangers, people who don't know the real me. I could totally reinvent myself. Be whoever I wanted to be. I could demand they call me Ann, tell them I'm the most popular girl at my school, and win the attention of all the hot boys within hours of my arrival.

Though I doubted any of that would really happen. Just because I'm with people who don't know me doesn't mean my real self won't make an immediate appearance. It's hard for me to open up to new people. Plus, I really don't like it when someone calls me Ann—I think Annie's a much cuter name. And I've never gotten the attention of a hot boy in my entire life. Well, I have—hello, Wade Johnson—but that was *unwanted* attention. *That* I'm great at.

I'd like to change that particularly annoying trait of mine.

Okay, I'm not drop-dead gorgeous with a bubbly, flirtatious personality, not by a long shot. I'm not a hideous troll, either, but come on. Hot guys have never noticed me— unless they're six and I'm blowing snot bubbles out my nose. Or I write really bad poetry that makes adolescent boys howl with laughter. And that's not the way I want boys to notice me.

"I'll be fine," I reassured Mom, offering her a smile in return, which somehow only seemed to upset her more. Her chin got all wobbly, and she yanked me into her arms, holding me close. I let her smother me with Mom love for a few minutes before I disentangled myself from her embrace. "Seriously, it's going to be okay. I'll write you and Dad as much as I can."

"Which shouldn't be very much at all. I want you to meet new people and try new things. You need to stay busy and have fun. Don't worry about us." She wagged her finger at me before her hand dropped to her side. "I know you feel a little stifled here, so this will be good for you."

Mom understood. She always had. We moved here when I was two, back to Dad's hometown; he felt right at home because he *was* home. Mom, on the other hand, was still considered an outsider, and they'd always treated her that way. So she knew what it was like, to feel like you didn't fit in. She understood my problems at school, when Dad always blew them off. Not that he was mean about it. He just didn't get it.

"It's going to be great," I told Mom with a genuine smile. My heart did a funny little flip in the center of my chest and I breathed deeply, telling myself everything really would be great.

Going to camp was going to change my life.

• • •

JAKE

*One month earlier*

"You're going. I know this is a last-minute decision and you're probably pissed that you have to leave tomorrow, but too damn bad, Jacob. You're out of here." Dad's voice was firm, simmering with anger. His eyes blazed with barely withheld fury as he glared at me. He was super pissed, but what else was new? "And that's final. No arguments, no defiance, no threats that you'll run away. The second you leave this house without my permission, I'm calling the cops. And they *will* lock you up. Thanks to your latest mishap, that's guaranteed."

I stared at him, my arms crossed in front of my chest, my jaw clenched so tight I felt like I could crush my teeth into powder. My uncle's summer camp held good memories. Back when I was a kid and had no cares in the world, and my main priorities had been swimming in the lake and hanging out with friends.

But those days were a long time ago.

Now I didn't want to go back. There was no point. I was a different person. Not just older, but freaking wiser.

Well. Maybe not wiser. I kept fucking up, like I couldn't help myself. That latest mishap Dad was talking about? Stealing hubcaps off fancy cars in the middle of the night with my so-called friends. We'd been drinking. I'd been dared. The moment the cops showed up, they all bailed on me. Every last one of them, and I was royally busted. They booked me like a real criminal, taking my photo, getting my fingerprints. I'd nearly pissed my pants I was so scared.

Never let them see it, though. Just kept my mouth shut and glared at everyone. When Dad showed up to bail me out, I almost went weak with relief. I believed I was home free— until he got me into the car and proceeded to yell the entire drive home.

That was the first clue that I'd have to finally pay for my sins.

Dad went with me to my court appearance and asked to speak to the judge. I thought he would plead my case. Tell the scowling middle-aged woman with glasses perched on the tip of her nose that I really was a good kid. I just needed another chance.

Nope. Dad chucked me so far under the bus, I still have tire marks across my stomach. He told the judge I was a screwup, a failure, a disappointment, and that he was afraid for my future. He then promised her if she gave me community service, he'd make sure I did my time by working at my uncle's summer camp under strict supervision.

She'd agreed.

And now here I am, going to camp and having to work with a bunch of asshole kids who'll give me nothing but crap over the next two months. The only thing that was giving me hope?

The possibility there would be plenty of pretty counselors with a bad-boy fetish. I'll be willing to fulfill whatever fantasy they have, as long as we can do it on the down low. My uncle gets one whiff of me doing something wrong, and I'm a dead man. I'll end up in juvenile hall or, worse, in freaking jail. My dad'll make sure I pay for my mistakes.

"Fine," I muttered, dropping my head so I didn't have to look him in the eye. Seeing the disappointment there, all the anger and frustration, I couldn't take it anymore. "I'll go."

His deep sigh of relief was loud, and hearing it didn't make me feel any better. We sat in the living room, Dad in his recliner, me on the couch. I let my arms drop to my sides and took a deep breath, glancing around the room. It was small, narrow, no pictures on the wall, no homey touches. A total bachelor pad, Dad had told me when we moved in to the place, like that was going to appeal to fourteen-year-old me.

After Mom died, Dad sold our house—too full of memories, he'd said, his expression pained—and we rented this shitty little two-story condo. A temporary move, he'd reassured me. The place was old but centrally located in single-dom paradise. As in, there were plenty of divorced women who lived in this complex who were hot for my dad.

And it sucked. Mom's dying had completely messed with my head. But Dad's moving us away from the only home I'd ever known had pushed me over the edge. The more trouble I got into, the more attention I received. It didn't matter if it was bad or good; at least someone was looking at me. Acknowledging me. Telling me I mattered.

Sort of.

"Spending the summer with your uncle Bob is just what you need," Dad said, his expression softening, the anger slowly dissipating because I didn't protest or get angry. Why fight it? At least at camp, I'd have some freedom.

I'd be working my ass off and under Uncle Bob's thumb

all the time, but what else could I do?

"Though just because you're surrounded by a bunch of young girls doesn't mean you should *touch* any of them." The pointed look Dad sent my way almost made me want to laugh.

Almost.

"They're off-limits. Forbidden. The campers, at least. You have to follow your uncle's rules. The counselors, they're your peers, but I wouldn't recommend you messing around with any of them, either. You don't need the distraction." He paused. "You mess up once, and you'll end up in juvie. Understand?"

I nodded. Whatever. I'd mess around with whoever I wanted, whenever I wanted. I'd freaking need the distraction so I wouldn't lose my mind having to work for Uncle Bob all summer long.

"You'll get out of here." *Away from my friends.* "You'll meet new people." *Who aren't my friends.* "You'll earn a little money and save it up." *So I can buy my own cigarettes or weed or whatever I want and not have to ask for cash from you.* "And you might learn a thing or two."

Yeah, right.

But instead of saying any of that, I nodded like I agreed and stood, finally meeting his gaze. His eyes weren't blazing with so much frustration anymore, and I felt like I'd jumped over the first hurdle. "I'd better go pack, then," I told him, and left the room.

Never looked back once, either.

# Chapter Two

## Annie

The bus ride was long, the road twisty enough to make my stomach pitch and roll like I was on a boat in the middle of an ocean storm. I tried to ignore it by slipping in my earbuds and closing my eyes, concentrating on my newly created playlist on my old iPod Touch, but it was no use. I ended up nauseous and trying my best not to hurl by the time the bus arrived at camp.

I was pretty sure it wasn't just the ride that made me sick to my stomach, though. I was super nervous, too. What if I had a hard time making friends? What if I couldn't open up? Back at school, I was known for being shy. Quiet. I kept to myself, kept my head down, got good grades.

In other words, I was totally boring. My guidance counselor told me as much when I met with her right before school ended.

"You're such a bright girl, but grades alone won't get you into the college of your choice," she'd reminded me. "They want someone well-rounded. A student who's both smart and social—the total package."

"The total package." Those words struck fear in my heart because I knew without a doubt I'm not the total package. Not by a long shot.

I was just…me.

Well, this was the summer of freedom. Of bravery. I needed to prove to myself that I could be more than just…me. I could become the total package and go back to school ready to conquer all. Join clubs, maintain my GPA, and maybe even lead a cheer.

Okay. That last one might be a stretch, but I could probably lead the school, right? Join student council? I'd always wanted to do that but figured I wasn't popular enough.

Summer camp was the perfect place to put my newfound bravery to work. How many books had I read where the nerdy girl went away to summer camp, transformed herself, made a ton of new friends, and got the hottest guy by the end of the summer? Too many to mention, and every one of those stories made me sigh with longing when I finished.

I wanted to be that girl. I wanted to be brave, make friends, accomplish something that I've always been too scared to do, and I wanted to end up with the hottest guy at camp by the end of the summer. I could do it.

Seriously. I could.

A very official-looking girl who couldn't be much older than me stood by the flagpole holding a clipboard, a whistle on a cord hanging around her neck. Her hair was a glossy brown and hung perfectly straight just to her shoulders. She wore a T-shirt with the camp emblem on the front, and she smiled as everyone milled around, not appearing fazed by all the loud chatter and squeals, girls hugging each other like they were long-lost friends finally reunited.

Like a loser, I stood there completely alone. For my age,

I knew I was late in going to summer camp, and it looked like everyone else had already been coming here for ages. Plus, I was here for only the second session, so I was totally late to the party.

As I glanced around and saw girls and boys breaking off into groups of three and four, I was one of the only girls with no one to talk to. My instant reaction was to retreat. The old me would've stood beneath a tree with my earbuds in and my music loud, my gaze glued to my ancient iPod—no phones worked up here since the reception was bad—like I was alone on purpose.

But the new me, the daring and brave me, lifted her chin, contemplating the group of girls standing the closest. They were all really pretty with perfect hair and makeup, wearing cute clothes I could only dream of affording. I took a hesitant step, then another one, ready to approach them, when someone tapped me on the shoulder.

I turned to find a very tall, very thin girl standing in front of me, a friendly smile stretching her mouth wide, her dark brown eyes meeting mine. "Hi!" she chirped, like I should know exactly who she is. "It's been *sooo* long, right?"

Frowning, I answered, "Sure?" Was she messing with me or what?

"I mean, it feels like I haven't been here in forever. And then I see you." She paused, as if waiting for me to answer with my name.

So I do.

"Annie."

"Right! Annie." She nodded, her smile growing wider. "Anyway, *Annie*. It's so freaking good to see you again. I've been waiting all year for our reunion." She pulled me into her arms, hugging me tightly, and I had no choice but to hug her back.

"Um, I missed you, too…" My voice drifted and I worried

for a moment that this girl could be a total wack job. Or she was playing a trick on me.

"Kelsey." She pulled away from me, her hands still gripping my shoulders. "I'm sorry I never wrote. I lost your address."

"More like you never had it," I reminded her.

Her nose scrunched up, drawing my attention to the many freckles covering it. "Well, you've always been a little selfish when it comes to revealing your true self."

This girl was more on point than she realized. "You know I'm a private person," I said with a smile.

"Right. I get it. I do. This is why we're the best of camp friends." Kelsey started to laugh and gave my shoulders a little shake. "I scare you, don't I?"

"Sort of," I admitted, which only made her laugh harder.

"I was just messing with you. Everyone's having their reunion moments and I was feeling like a total dork. I saw you standing by yourself looking like a dork, too, so I thought I'd break the ice." Kelsey let go of my shoulders and her laughter faded, though the smile was still firmly in place. "You're really Annie?"

Wow. I'm impressed with this girl's bravery. I sort of love it. Maybe I could learn a thing or two from her. "Yeah. And you're really Kelsey?"

"Yep." She stood taller, which was saying something because the girl was like, twice as tall as me. "How old are you?"

"Sixteen."

"Me, too! That means we'll probably be in the same cabin. We should share a bunk! What do you prefer? Top or bottom?"

"Um, top?" Normally I'd want the bottom, too afraid I might roll over in my sleep and fall off the top. My grandma always said it looked like I wrestled alligators in my sleep, I tangled up the sheets and comforter so much.

"Perfect. I prefer the bottom. I'm too tall; I'll knock my head into the ceiling." She grinned, looking rather pleased with herself. "We're like long-lost reunited camp friends, together again, right?" Before I could reply, she slung her arm around my shoulders and steered me so we were facing the girl at the flagpole, whose cheery veneer was starting to slip a little. "Bet you ten bucks she's going to blow that whistle as loud as she can in the next five minutes."

"Can't take the bet, since I agree with you," I said as Kelsey dropped her arm from around my shoulders. "She literally looks ready to blow. Her face is red and everything."

Kelsey laughed. "You're funny."

I thought that was pretty amusing, considering she was the one who forged a fake friendship with me in a matter of minutes. "So are you."

She tucked a wild strand of deep auburn hair behind her ear. "I think we're going to get along just fine. Though you've been warned—sometimes I act a little crazy."

*No kidding*, I wanted to say but didn't. Instead I told her, "So do I." It was a lie, but I wanted it to be true.

Kelsey nodded, looking pleased. "We're going to make a perfect team."

We waited for Clipboard Girl to blow her whistle, getting jostled again and again by people passing by as we chatted about nothing at all. I couldn't believe how quickly I'd just made a friend.

Maybe I really *could* be brave Annie this summer.


"This is our cabin." Our counselor, Hannah, stood on the front porch with a smile before pushing open the creaky door and waving a hand for us to go inside. "Everyone choose your bunk first! Then we'll introduce ourselves, put away our stuff real quick, and get ready. We're going down to the lake in thirty minutes, so we have to hurry!"

Hannah's words froze me and I couldn't move, though every other girl assigned to G7A pushed past me, knocking into me with their duffel bags, trying to get their preferred bunk before anyone else. I couldn't believe it. First day here and we were already expected to go swimming? I thought we'd ease into it. Or they'd give us the option and I'd just never have to make that choice. I didn't want everyone to know I couldn't swim on the first day we were here. Talk about humiliating.

"Annie! Come here!" Kelsey waved me over to the bunk she was standing next to, and I went to join her, dropping my heavy bag on the floor beside me. We had to make the trek to our cabin carrying our own bags, and since the senior girls' cabins were the farthest ones out, we had the longest hike. I was freaking exhausted. Hiking was not my thing. Being outdoors really wasn't my thing, either.

"This is ours. What do you think? You're still cool with sleeping on the top bunk?" Kelsey asked hopefully.

I nodded, not sure I had any strength left to climb the short ladder that led up to my bed. And I wanted to lie down more than anything.

"Girls!" Hannah clapped her hands and everyone went quiet. "Please say your name, how long you've been coming here, and what you're looking forward to most while you're at camp." She nodded at a tall, dark-haired girl. "You go first."

They all each said their names: Hailey, Kaycee, Caitie, Presley, Bobbee, and Gwen. And what they were most looking forward to: swimming, spending time with their old friends, and hanging out with cute boys.

Seriously. They all said pretty much the same thing. And as for cute boys? I saw plenty of them, including one with dark hair and a scowl on his face as he helped out the camp director. All the girls talked about him on the hike over to our cabin, going on and on about how cute he was and how he really didn't talk to them. I could tell they'd known one another for years. They'd all been coming to Camp Pine Ridge for a long time and had a strong bond.

"I'm Kelsey," my new friend announced, smiling at everyone. "This is my second year here and I'm looking forward to making new friends." She looked at me. "And going on new adventures."

I smiled in return. It was like Kelsey spoke my language, I swear.

"And last but not least, let's hear from our newest member of W7A." Hannah leaned in closer to me. "We take offense to the *G* standing for girls. So we substitute it with *W* for women."

"Oh, I get it." I sounded so lame.

They all smiled at me, waiting for my introduction.

Clearing my throat, I said, "My name is Annie, and as Hannah said, this is my first year at Camp Pine Ridge. The things I'm most looking forward to are soaking up the camp experience, meeting new friends, and learning how to make a lanyard."

They all laughed, which was exactly the reaction I'd been looking for. Blushing, I turned back to my bunk, gazing longingly at the mattress that awaited me. I was so tired, but the afternoon had only just begun.

"Okay everyone, now that's done, listen up! Put your bags over here." Hannah pointed to an alcove where there was one solid wall of nothing but cubbies. Everyone was talking so fast and so loudly I didn't think anyone was really paying any attention to what she was saying. "You're each assigned cubbies. Your names are already on them, so just stash your bags under the table in the corner when you're finished unpacking." Hannah clapped again. "You have about fifteen minutes before we leave, so hurry!"

"We have to unpack and be ready to go to the lake in fifteen minutes?" Kelsey asked me under her breath. "After making that hike? She can keep on dreaming."

"No kidding," I muttered. I'd never been a fan of PE. I didn't play any organized sports. I never really thought I was out of shape, but I guess I never really thought about my shape, period. I bet I wouldn't have any problem falling asleep tonight, and I'd sort of worried about that.

When it came to going to camp, I worried about pretty much everything once I got on the bus and we pulled out of the parking lot, my parents still standing there watching us drive away. All my adventurous, *I'm going to turn myself into a new person* plans faded the farther away I got from home. There was no turning back now. All my old insecurities flared up, reminding me of all the things I didn't like to do. All of the things I was most afraid of.

Like swimming.

And water.

My mom asked me if I was sure about going to a camp that was literally based around a lake. They were even well known for their water activities. But I figured I'd be able to avoid the water and focus on the arts and crafts stuff.

"They're not going to like, make us swim or anything, are they?"

Kelsey shrugged. "I doubt it. Though who knows? They might just toss us off the dock and tell us to start kicking." She grinned.

I was secretly horrified. That sounded like a nightmare, like the absolute worst thing that could ever happen to me.

But I returned Kelsey's smile and told myself I wasn't going to let anything bother me. I was here. It was my first day at camp.

I was determined to have a good time.

• • •

## JAKE

"The new campers seem all right," my uncle Bob said as we walked toward the lake together. I didn't get a chance to go home to my dad's over the holiday break between sessions. I ended up spending the Fourth of July hanging out with a few other counselors I'd become friends with since I'd been here. We had a barbecue in the afternoon under the hot blazing sun, and Betsy from the dining hall made her famous potato salad. We hung out in the lake, considering it was too hot to do anything else, and later that night we lit fireworks, sending them high into the sky before they landed in the water with a sizzling hiss.

We had fun. I flirted hard-core with Lacey, one of the counselors for the senior girls. She's cute and she seems sort of into me, but I wasn't sure if I wanted to pursue anything with her, especially when we were stuck together until August. What if we got sick of each other? I didn't want to take the chance, and while Uncle Bob didn't necessarily say I couldn't "date"—his word choice—any of the counselors, I knew he wasn't big on it, either.

Every other counselor was pairing off with someone, but I felt like I couldn't. Sucked being related to the guy. Oh, and his knowledge of my rebellious past didn't help, either.

"Yeah." I knew he expected me to answer, even though I didn't really know what to say. Another group of kids had come in, big deal. This meant I'd had to put in real sweat work the last couple of days, cleaning up the grounds, helping paint the dining hall, a project that they never got around to in the spring.

That had been major work. I collapsed into bed every

night and slept like the dead. I was still tired and I had to be on my A game, since all those new campers were probably headed straight for the lake, it was so hot.

"There are no activities planned this afternoon, so there'll be water time instead." Uncle Bob smiled, resting his hands on his hips. He had on a Camp Pine Ridge T-shirt and I could see tufts of hair sticking up around the neckline. If I still stood a chance of inheriting his hairiness, I'd be investing in wax.

"Right." I knew I was on water patrol. I'd need to sneak an energy drink before I went out there.

"The big spaghetti feed is tonight, and afterward the kids will be participating in get-to-know-you activities. Bonds all the kids within their cabin groups." He smiled and nodded. "Never fails, even after all these years."

"Uh-huh." He was talking to me like I hadn't been here so far this summer, but that was just his way. He liked to recite lists, go over everything that was on his mind by saying it out loud. Whatever worked, right? He was quirky, but everyone loved my uncle. They even called him Fozzie Bear because he was so hairy—and our last name was Fazio. I'd even slipped up and called him Fozzie once or twice, though that was strictly a camp nickname. He'd probably kill me if I called him Uncle Fozzie Bear at Thanksgiving.

"You'll be at the spaghetti feed, right?" He turned to look at me, his sharp gaze making me feel like I probably did something wrong. I racked my brain, trying to remember if I'd screwed up somehow in the last few days, but I came up empty.

"I'll be there. I wouldn't miss Cook Betsy's spaghetti for the world." It was pretty delicious, like most everything she made. Nothing like my mom's, but no one could beat her cooking, ever.

We stopped near the dock, the both of us staring out at the lake. It was a beautiful but hot day. Nothing but blue skies dotted with puffy white clouds that looked like cotton balls, and the water sparkled and shone from the reflection of the sun. As a kid, this had been my absolute favorite spot. Now it felt kinda like prison, considering I was forced to come work here. It was hard to find any positives to this situation.

"I'll see you there tonight, then," Uncle Bob continued. "For now, I'll need you and Dane working double duty here. I figure the kids are going to be flocking to the water for the entire session, considering it's the hottest time of the year."

As if on cue, we could hear them coming for the lake, a low rumbling in the distance like a herd of animals just set free and ready to make their escape. We both turned to watch the older cabin groups headed our way and being led by their counselors. Dane, the head lifeguard for the lakefront, stood at the water's edge by the canoes and kayaks, which were docked and ready for anyone to take out on the water.

"Ah, here they are. We'd better get to work." He clapped me on the shoulder, his gaze dropping to my swim trunks. "Good to see you wearing the red shorts. You'll get tower duty while I keep Dane on the ground. He does better with the ladies. You're too grumpy." With a wink and a smile, my uncle strolled away, yelling out his greetings at the kids who were running toward the water. They all chorused back, "Hi, Fozzie Bear!" at the top of their lungs.

Grimacing, I headed off the dock and toward the lifeguard tower.

Summer felt like it was never going to end.

# Chapter Three

"Hey, Pine Ridge campers, listen up!"

I wanted to groan. Here came Uncle Bob and his giant red-and-white megaphone. His deep voice felt like it could rattle the walls when he screamed into that thing in the dining hall. The place was packed. Everyone was eating dinner and talking so loudly I could hardly hear myself think. But the minute he went to the front of the building, turned his precious megaphone on, and we all heard the squealing feedback?

Everyone went dead silent.

"For some of us, it's our first night here! How's everyone feeling?" He waved his free hand up, encouraging everyone to say something.

The entire dining hall erupted in cheering. Even Brian, the junior counselor in charge of cabin B7B, was going along with it, and he was almost as sarcastic and jaded as me. This was why we'd become such good friends.

"Okay, okay, simmer down." Uncle Bob pulled the

megaphone away from his mouth and grinned at everyone before he launched into his speech. "My name is Fozzie Bear and I am your camp director." He did a dead-on imitation of the beloved Muppet, and there was plenty of laughter.

My uncle was the ultimate performer.

"How's the spaghetti dinner, huh? Can we all give a rousing cheer to Cook Betsy?" Everyone cheered, even me, though I was a little reluctant.

"Yeah, Betsy! We love you!" He made kissy noises through the megaphone, which sounded horrible. "All right, then. I know you're excited to welcome the new batch of summer friends. But don't forget we're all meeting out by the bonfire pit at eight o'clock sharp! There will be a special skit that was put together by your favorite camp counselors, so get excited, kids! It's gonna be epic!"

"Your uncle says everything's epic," Brian muttered to me, and I nodded my reply. "Epic" was currently Uncle Bob's favorite word.

He made a few more short announcements and then turned off the megaphone, indicating that he was done. I resumed eating, trying to figure out a way to avoid going to the bonfire pit, when I felt someone come up behind me.

"Hey." I glanced over my shoulder to find Lacey standing next to our table, a sexy smile curving her pink-glossed lips. "How are you?" she asked.

"Good. How are you?" I said absently, my gaze snagging on a blond head. I'd always had a thing for blondes. This one was a camper with her hair in a ponytail, and it was constantly bouncing up and down, her hair swinging with every flick of her head.

She burst out laughing, and the sound was nothing but pure happiness.

My heart panged, which was stupid. But I didn't remember the last time I felt like that. Happy. Carefree.

"I'm great." Lacey's gaze drifted over me, her lids heavy as she flicked her hair behind her shoulder. My supposed interest in her went totally against type. I'd spent time with Lacey because I was bored and it was something to do. I knew that made me a total asshole but hey, I was embracing it. "So what are you up to tonight?"

Brian nudged me in the ribs, a giant grin on his face. I tried my best to ignore him.

"Not much," I said, keeping my tone casual as my gaze kept following the blonde. She turned to her right, her gaze snagging on mine for the briefest moment. Her smile was big, her joy radiating all over her face, and our eyes locked for the briefest moment.

I looked away, refocused on Lacey. I couldn't let myself get interested in the blonde—a camper. No way. That was going against the rules, and Uncle Bob wouldn't let me get away with shit.

"We should hang together tonight. Later. After the skit," she said.

Huh. I wished we could go somewhere during the skit. The camp introductory night brought out the worst in my uncle, where he sang the cheesiest songs completely off-key and the counselors put together a special skit welcoming everyone to camp. I'd already seen it with the first session, and I really wasn't in the mood to see it again. Though the kids seemed to love it. Luckily enough, I didn't have to participate.

"Sounds good," I said nonchalantly. "What time are you thinking?"

"I don't know, after lights-out?" Lights-out was ten o'clock, but all the counselors were free once the kids fell asleep. Mostly. Sometimes the older campers sneaked out, too, though none of the counselors ever busted them. "Maybe around eleven?" She tilted her head to the side, her hair spilling over her shoulder, her gaze knowing. She was hot and she knew it, with her long dark hair and those equally dark eyes.

I should say no. Lacey looked like trouble. But I'd always had a thing for trouble, so I found myself saying, "Out by the volleyball court?" That was code for star-gazing, which was also code for making out.

Her smile grew and she nodded. "See you then." With that, she turned and went back to her table.

"Nice," Brian said once she was out of earshot. He jabbed me in the ribs with his elbow again. "Looks like someone's getting laid tonight."

"Don't jump to conclusions." I doubted I'd get laid. But there were plenty of other things we could do to pass the time.

And I was looking forward to doing each and every one of those things, too.

. . .

## Annie

"Okay, it works like this." Hannah smiled at Kelsey and me, as we were the ones sitting directly across from her. She was trying to show me the ropes, since this was my first time at camp, and Kelsey was just along for the ride. She'd glommed on to me like she had no other friends here, and I was starting to think that was true. The other girls in our cabin sat at the table with us, and while they seemed friendly enough, they had their own core group.

Leaving Kelsey and me on the outside looking in.

"Every day, I assign someone to be the one who goes and fetches our food for each meal. It's a rotating schedule. Tonight, I'll get everyone's food. Tomorrow it's someone else's turn and so on. The schedule is on the bathroom wall in the cabin, so make sure and check it so you know when it's your turn. Okay?" Hannah smiled at the both of us and we nodded. "I'll be right back."

"She's really nice," Kelsey said after Hannah left. "Way better than Lacey."

"Who's Lacey?" I didn't want to be excluded from the rest of the table's conversation, but the other girls were scooted close together, their heads bent as they gossiped about Jake, the same dark-haired boy they'd all gone on about earlier. I heard lots of giggling and exaggerated descriptions of his hotness, and I really wanted in on that conversation.

"The other counselor for our age group. There are two cabins full of sixteen-year-old girls. Lacey was my counselor last year, and she's a total bitch." Kelsey waved her hand in a dismissive gesture. "Just be glad she's not our counselor."

Hannah came back to the table multiple times with our plates and food before we were all finally able to dig in. The other girls talked to us finally, Hailey being the most friendly, and we all had a good laugh over our names all ending with an "ee" sound—with the exception of Gwen. Not that it seemed to bother her. She was calm yet friendly, and she seemed to be unfazed by just about anything.

Once we started all chatting together as we ate spaghetti, I realized everyone in my group seemed to have a super talent. Kaycee was an excellent softball player who was on her way to a full scholarship in college. Hailey was an excellent singer. Presley was an actress and was big in the drama club at her high school—I noticed her flair for drama, so that was no surprise. Caitie played soccer, and Bobbee was a dancer. She and Gwen had been putting together a routine for the end-of-summer talent show for six years running, and they were already eager to come up with something new.

"What about you?" I asked Kelsey. "What do you like to do?"

Kelsey shrugged and pushed her empty tray away from her. "You'll laugh."

"No, we won't," Bobbee was quick to say. "We're nice. I promise."

The other girls laughed, and I winced. I hoped they weren't laughing at Kelsey. That wouldn't be nice. I wanted to like these girls, not feel like I ended up with a bunch of possible bullies.

"I'm on the debate team at school," Kelsey admitted, wrinkling her nose.

"Well, that's cool," Hailey said. "I'm on the academic pentathlon team at my school. I have been since seventh grade."

"Nerd," Gwen murmured, making everyone giggle.

"So does this mean you're really great at arguing?" Presley asked.

Kelsey nodded. "I could convince you to do just about anything if I set my mind to it."

"What about you, Annie?" Caitie asked, her eyes sparkling as her gaze met mine. "What's your superpower?"

What could I say? That I was a really great reader? That sounded lame, though it was the truth. I could read a book a day, even when I had to be at school and had homework. But that wasn't really a skill. Nothing I did could be considered a skill. I wasn't really part of any groups at school. I had nothing.

"Hey, chicas."

My entire table forgot Caitie's question when they set eyes on the boy who'd just stopped by our table. When I turned to see who it was, I sort of forgot, too.

Okay, my mind went completely blank, because the hottest boy I'd ever set eyes on stood just behind Kaycee, a sly smile curving his lips as he flipped his slightly shaggy golden-brown hair out of his eyes. "Hey, Kyle," they all singsonged.

"What's going on? Ready to watch Fozzie Bear make an ass out of himself tonight?" Kyle laughed and the girls giggled.

"I think it's adorable, how he gets up on stage and

humiliates himself by singing really awful songs," Gwen said. "When I was eight I thought he was the coolest thing ever."

"Me, too," Presley agreed, her gaze glued to Kyle.

My gaze was glued to Kyle, too. I couldn't help it. He was by far the handsomest boy I'd ever been this close to, like, ever.

"Yeah, well, I think he's lame as hell." He flicked his head again, and it almost felt like a practiced move, probably because he had to do it all the time. Why didn't he just get a haircut? "We should all sit next to each other."

"That would be awesome," Caitie said, sounding cool, though I could see the excitement in her eyes as she looked at all of us real quick before she turned to face Kyle. "You guys should save us a spot."

"Will do. See ya." He waved and sauntered back to his table, where he proceeded to high-five every single boy sitting there.

"Oh. My. God." Kaycee fanned herself. "Did he get hotter over the winter, or what?"

"Every summer it's worse," Bobbee said. "As in, he gets better-looking and it drives us all right out of our minds."

The girls erupted in laughter, chiming in with their agreement.

"Who is he?" I couldn't help but ask, earning curious looks from every girl at our table.

"Only the most popular boy at camp," Presley said. "He's been coming for second session for what feels like forever and I swear, he's gone out with every single one of us at least once, right, girls?"

Gwen nodded, her lips twisting as she scanned all of us crowded around the rickety table. "Definitely, especially during our middle school years." Her smirk grew. "Let me ask an important question. Who here at this table has kissed Kyle?"

Six hands shot into the air, with the exception of Kelsey and me.

I looked to my right to find a boy watching me. The dark-haired one everyone had been talking about earlier. The camp director's nephew, Jacob. He was cute, too. Not classically handsome like Kyle, but he had that brooding, loner look going for him.

And that was sort of hot. I could see why the girls went on about him, too.

"What do you think of Kyle, Annie?" Bobbee asked, nudging me in the side to get my attention.

Way to put me on the spot. "Um, he's all right."

They all laughed, and for a fleeting moment, I thought they were laughing at me. But then I realized they were laughing at the absurdity of my words.

Because seriously, we all thought Kyle was better than all right. Did we want to necessarily admit that out loud?

Probably not.

# Chapter Four

Four days into camp, and I'd come to some realizations.

Summer camp is just as clichéd as I wished it to be. And this wasn't an insult, either. I liked the fact that the camp director was sort of odd and crazy yet lovable. That Nancy, the lady who ran the arts and crafts building, believed she was a hippie and wore flowing skirts and flowers in her hair. That all the boys checked out all the girls and the little kids ran circles around us every night no matter what we were trying to do, and that our bathroom looked like a girl bomb exploded inside and that our counselor Hannah left every night after lights-out so she could go hook up with Brian, one of the counselors for the teen boys' cabins.

That last bit of gossip I'd just learned over breakfast. Presley told all of us as we ate eggs and bacon and hash browns. Well, some of us were eating fruit and yogurt—Gwen and Bobbee—because they didn't want to start their day off with "nothing but fat and carbs "—direct quote.

"She waits about fifteen or twenty minutes before she leaves," Presley said, her eyes wide as she watched us, the knowing look on her face saying it all. "So last night I decided to follow her."

"You did not," Hailey practically squealed.

Presley shushed her, and Kaycee clapped her hand over Hailey's mouth. "I did, too," Presley said proudly. "She went to the dock and there was Brian waiting for her. They sat together on the edge, right over the lake, and when they started kissing, that's when I practically fell into a bush. They heard me and I had to run away because I swear, Brian was standing up and ready to investigate. What if he'd found me?"

They all started to laugh, and so did I. Kelsey just picked at her hash browns and I wondered what was up. The girls hadn't fully embraced us into their inner circle yet, but they weren't rude, either. I figured it would take some time, and I was fine with that.

Maybe Kelsey wasn't.

There was more gossip to be had, and I listened with rapt attention, waiting for any mention of Kyle. Dreamy, handsome, slightly-cocky-but-who-could-blame-him Kyle, with his sweet lopsided smile and his sparkling hazel eyes and the way he'd always say hi to me when we passed each other. It made me want to walk past him all the time, just so I could hear his deep voice say hey or hi, always calling me "new girl."

Like when he gave me the chin lift and a quick "what's up, new girl" as he jogged by. Then he stopped and asked if I knew the time and I said I didn't and he said "oh, that's cool" just before he smiled and left me. I'd stood frozen in the middle of the trail for what felt like forever, a bunch of ten-year-olds running past screaming at the top of their lungs finally snapping me out of my Kyle-induced haze.

Okay, fine, I had it bad for Kyle. Problem? He barely knew I existed. I figured I would stick out like a sore thumb, considering I was the new girl among girls he'd gone to camp with for years, but it actually turned out to be a good thing. I was the girl who never liked the spotlight before, but at camp, it was totally to my advantage. The boys all asked about me, with the exception of Fozzie Bear's nephew, Jacob.

He avoided all of us like the plague. I was fairly certain the girls tried to chat him up at one point or another over the last four days, but he wouldn't give. Not even crack a smile, which just infuriated them. And then spurred them all to try even harder.

It was kind of amusing to watch, though I never participated. He...scared me, in a way. There was this intensity about him, like he could see right through all of us. Right through me. That he knew my bravery was a facade, that I was really nothing more than a weak little girl falling into line, trying my hardest to make friends.

Or maybe that was my own fears. I don't know.

"We're going to the dock tonight," Gwen told me as she guided me into the bathroom later that afternoon. The other girls followed after her. "The boys are meeting us there after lights-out. And you're coming with us."

"Why?" I didn't know how to say that I was scared to go out on the dock. What if it collapsed and we all fell into the water? God, I'd probably drown. My entire body trembled just thinking about it.

"Because all the boys will be there, including Kyle." Gwen got right in my face and smiled. "It's the perfect opportunity for you two to get to know each other better."

I wasn't sure about that, but I wasn't going to argue.

Gwen grabbed her caddy full of makeup and started going through everything. "I'm going to give you a makeover," she told me.

Excitement rose inside me, despite my worry about the dock. Gwen was the makeup guru of the cabin. She could transform any of the girls with her expertise. "You don't have to…" I started to protest, but she shook her head.

"Nope, I'm so doing it. This will be fun."

This summer, I'd wanted to belong to something bigger than me. And I felt like my girls—excuse me, my *women*—in cabin W7A were already becoming my gang. My posse. My squad.

Whatever I should call them, I believed they were my friends, and I wanted to get to know them better. They were fun. They didn't push me or make me feel dumb for my preference of learning the fine art of lanyards over going swimming or hanging out at the lake in my bikini. Though I did bring bikinis with me. A bunch of them. I refused to bring a one-piece swimsuit for fear that would be all I wore all summer. Not that I'd hung out around the water much yet.

Yeah, I'd sort of failed that summer bucket list item so far.

I frowned as Gwen riffled through her cosmetics, searching for the right colors that would suit my skin tone, she'd told me. Did they make fun of me behind my back? Sometimes I wondered if they found me amusing and that's why they kept me around.

That was a depressing thought. One I didn't want to focus on.

"Bobbee is going to help you with your outfit for later." Gwen stopped just in front of me. "Close your eyes."

I did as she asked, pressing my lips together as I felt the brush start to feather over my eyelid. "What's later?"

Gwen let out an exasperated sigh. "The dock, remember? We're going to wait until Hannah sneaks out with Brian, and then we're all going to the lake."

"But don't Hannah and Brian meet on the dock?"

Gwen started in on my other eyelid. "Presley overheard them talking earlier." All we ever seemed to do was spy on our counselor. If only Hannah knew. "They're meeting at the bonfire pit. It's s'mores night and Brian told Hannah he could keep the fire going long into the night."

I started to laugh, and so did Gwen. "That's so cheesy."

"I know, right? But Hannah said something like, 'Oh, I bet you could.' Those two are so hot for each other and camp's barely begun." Gwen started working on the first eyelid again. "Though we're second session, so maybe they've been together the entire summer. Who knows?"

Right. Who knows? Camp was fueled on gossip and speculation, and we hadn't heard anything about Hannah and Brian prior to our arriving. How could we? All kinds of stories buzzed from cabin to cabin, sights of people just hanging out together turning into a major event. *Are they into each other or not? Did they hook up? Are they fighting?* Our phones didn't work up here, so we were all social-media deprived. We'd turn anything to gossip, claiming we had the facts to back up the story when we had nothing but our vivid imaginations.

It seemed all in good fun. I hadn't heard any malicious stories.

Yet.

"What's the deal with the new guy?" Presley said as she strolled into the bathroom.

I cracked open my eyes when Gwen stepped away from me. "What new guy?"

Presley rolled her eyes. "The other lifeguard. The one we've all been trying to flirt with the last few days. Jacob or Jake or whatever."

Right. He was a lifeguard. Not that I would know, considering I never went to the lake.

"I don't know. He never talks," Gwen said as she grabbed a giant, fluffy brush and a compact of facial powder. She popped the compact open and dabbed the brush in the powder, gathering up so much my eyes went wide at the thought of all that powder being brushed onto my face.

I'd end up looking like a ghost.

"He's hot," Presley said, going to lean against the counter. "But he doesn't give me the time of day."

"He's not supposed to. They get in trouble for messing around with the campers," Gwen pointed out, sounding logical, which always seemed to infuriate Presley.

"Whatever. Like there are *never* any counselor/camper hookups here." Presley grinned. "Give me a break."

"From what I've heard, Fozzie doesn't want his nephew hooking up with anyone at camp. That goes for counselors, too." Gwen wielded the brush at me and swept it across my cheeks and forehead. "Rumor is he's a troublemaker who got busted by the cops for stealing."

"He's a criminal?" Presley rubbed her hands together. "Intriguing. How do you know all of this?"

Gwen shrugged and turned to face her. "I hang out a lot at the lake. I've heard stories."

"Hanging out, drooling over Dane?" Dane, the head lifeguard, was absolutely gorgeous, though way too old for all of us. What sealed the deal was his Australian accent. He only had to say a few words and girls were swooning left and right. Not me, though.

I didn't hang out with lifeguards.

"Whatever." No one really spoke about it, but we were all aware of Gwen's raging crush on Dane. The fact that he had a solid eight to ten years on Gwen wasn't a deterrent. She tried her best to gain his attention and though he gave it to her, it wasn't in the way she wanted. He patted her head and called her cute—this, according to Kaycee when she told me the story, infuriated Gwen. She'd hatched a plan to land him by the end of the summer.

We all figured she was in for a big disappointment.

"So…why are you guys helping me?" I asked as Gwen

feathered the compact brush across my cheeks. I appreciated that they wanted to make me over, but I also didn't really get it.

"Because you're our friend, silly. And we know you like Kyle," Presley said. I started to protest, but she just laughed. "Don't bother coming up with some lame excuse. You like him. It's okay. At one point or another, all of us have liked him, so it's expected. It's like a camp ritual."

Gwen and Presley laughed some more.

But I didn't.

Was it typical of me that I fell into line and crushed on Kyle like all the rest of the girls? I liked him for his looks and nothing else, considering I didn't really know him. So did that make me shallow? I wanted to get to know him better, but it was so hard. He was always with his friends. He hung out a lot at the pool or the lake. And I was never there.

I was too scared to go there.

"Is there, um..." My voice drifted off and I cleared my throat, my heart starting to pound when Gwen and Presley turned their curious gazes on me. "Is Kyle more than good-looking? Like, is he funny? Nice? Smart?"

Gwen winced. "Smart?" The look on her face said it all. Maybe not.

"He says dumb stuff, and that makes us laugh," Presley said like she was being helpful.

But that only made me feel worse.

"Listen, he's very nice. Entertaining," Gwen said, grabbing another makeup brush and waving it toward my face. "Now sit still. I need to finish your face. Pres, quit distracting her."

I let her work her magic, my mind racing with possibilities. Most of them negative, like my fear of water possibly causing me to freak out. I needed to stay strong. I needed to act like tonight was no big deal.

I'd embrace it. Embrace me. Tonight I was going to wear

makeup and a cute outfit and one of those bikinis I brought with me that still had the price tags on it and I was going to have fun. I was going to convince Kelsey to go with us and have fun, too. It could be done. It would be done.

I guaranteed it.

# Chapter Five

Everyone was out tonight.

I left the staff cabin around ten thirty to see a bunch of people milling about. More like sneaking around. I knew Brian and Hannah were meeting at the bonfire pit, so that wasn't happening. I didn't want to hang out on the volleyball court again. I wanted to go somewhere more private. Somewhere Lacey and I could really be alone.

Turning, I headed toward the lake, not surprised to see a small group clustered out on the dock, most of them sitting on the end, their legs swinging over the water. A girl squealed and soft laughter followed, but I ignored it. Most of them were around my age, but they were all campers. I couldn't really hang out with them, since Uncle Bob frowned upon it. I noticed Kyle was among the group, and we were cool, but he was kind of a dipshit, so yeah. Not someone I really wanted to be friends with for the long term.

Worked out well, then, that I couldn't.

I was about to go left when I collided with someone. A female someone, if the muffled "sorry" I heard was any indication. I grabbed hold of slender shoulders and set her away from me, surprise washing over me when I realized it was the new girl. The cute blonde with the swishing ponytail. I didn't recognize her at first, what with all the makeup she was wearing and the fact that her hair was down, waving past her shoulders.

"You shouldn't be out here," I tell her, my voice low, like a warning. Helplessly I ran my thumbs across her soft skin, catching just beneath the sleeves of her T-shirt.

She frowned, pulling out of my grip. I let my arms fall at my sides, surprised that my fingers were still tingling from... what? Touching her? That was insane.

"Seriously, I could write you up," I continued when she still said nothing. "You should go back to your cabin."

Her lips parted, and my gaze fell to them. They were full. And glossy. And...tempting? "You can't tell me what to do."

I jerked my gaze from her mouth, surprise filling me at her defiant tone. Her eyes bugged out, like she'd just shocked herself, before she turned and ran toward the dock, her hair streaming behind her.

What the hell just happened?

"Hey, lover boy."

I turned to see Lacey running up to me, nearly tackling me to the ground when she grabbed hold of me. She pressed her hand against the back of my neck and pulled me down for a kiss, but I broke away from her before our lips connected, taking a step back. "Not here, Lace," I muttered, looking around to make sure no one saw us.

Specifically the blonde that I just ran into. And thought about kissing.

Had I lost my mind or what?

She frowned, her lips forming a little glossy pout. "Why

do we have to meet in secret?"

"Aw, come on. Don't you think it's more fun that way?" I smiled, trying to convince her that what I said was true. I needed a distraction from the new girl, and Lacey could help with that.

But she just continued to pout, her hands on her hips as she glared at me. "It's all we do, Jake. Sneak around after lights-out just so we can what? Make out for ten minutes? Then you tell me you have to go to sleep and you end up ditching me. Every single time."

Damn, she was ruining my mood. "I just…I don't want anyone to catch us, you know? I can't have a bunch of gossip spread about me. About us," I added. I didn't want my uncle to find out I was doing this. He expected me to be some sort of example, which was laughable. And if I did something that pissed him off, he'd send me back to my dad—who'd send me back to court and that mean judge.

I didn't need that sort of trouble. I needed to stay clean. Or at least, look clean.

Messing around with Lacey would be bad enough. Having…thoughts about that new camper was way out of line. And they were just thoughts. You shouldn't be held accountable for thoughts, right?

"Well, everyone's out tonight so…what? You want to call this off?" She curled her arms in front of her chest and studied me, waiting for an answer. "I don't like being treated like a side piece."

"Oh, come on. Like you've seen me with anyone else around here?" I'd been working so hard I hadn't noticed anyone else—until tonight. The first week of camp with a new group was basically me running around at full speed and working from dawn until dusk. That I even made time to hang out with Lacey for a little bit was a big deal, not that she'd see it that way.

"I don't know, but you sure don't seem that interested in me." She lifted her chin. "I could find someone else, you know."

"Then go for it." I didn't need this. Not like we were a real couple. Funny, the sense of relief that suddenly flooded me. I didn't like being drilled, especially by a girl I'd never see again once the summer was over.

Lacey's gaze turned downright murderous. I bet she wasn't the sort of girl who dealt much with rejection. "Fine. I will." She stormed off, taking the same path the blonde just had and headed straight for the dock.

Rubbing the back of my neck, I watched her go, frustration making my stomach knot.

Women. They were freaking crazy.

• • •

## ANNIE

I stopped at the beginning of the dock, my breath coming in quick, sharp bursts. I wanted to look back and see if Jacob was still there. But then again, I didn't want him to see me checking for him, either. Would he assume I was scared by his threat? Or worse, that I liked him or something?

Because I so didn't. He freaked me out—and made me angry. Who did he think he was? My father? Trying to say he'll write me up or whatever? Everyone else was out tonight, but I was the one who would get in trouble?

I didn't think so.

"Annie!"

I glanced up to see Kelsey coming toward me. "Hey," I said weakly.

"Where were you?"

"I had to go to the bathroom." True, but I left out my running into Jacob. "Is Kyle here?" I asked, wincing the moment the words left my mouth. Could I be any more obvious?

"He is," Kelsey said with a nod. She hooked her arm through mine. "Let's go."

Hesitation made my feet stick to the creaky wooden slats, and I glanced down. The water swirled below; I could actually *see* it, and all I could think about was falling through the weak slats. Plunging into the water. I sucked in a sharp breath, and Kelsey sent me a weird look, tugging on my arm. "You okay?"

My throat was dry, and I could feel the panic setting in. I took a deep, shuddering breath and inwardly commanded myself to start walking. And I did.

On shaky legs.

Kelsey dragged me along, the other girls coming to greet me, their smiles wide, their voices enthusiastic. I was ready to feel on top of the world tonight, and the moment I saw Kyle, my heart started to pick up speed.

Of course, he was gorgeous. Of course, he was dressed perfectly, the white T-shirt showing off his tanned skin. He laughed at something Presley said, and I fought the wave of jealousy that threatened. They were old friends. They could talk and laugh, though I wished he were talking and laughing with me.

"Come on," Kelsey muttered as she took me over to where they stood. I said nothing, my brain scrambling to come up with something to say to Kyle.

"So hey. What happened?" Presley asked, her gaze on me. She had a tiny flask clasped in her hand, and she brought it to her lips, taking a big swig before handing it over to Kyle.

Shock coursed through me, though I didn't know why. I fully expected them to smuggle alcohol onto the premises. I'd heard them talking earlier and knew there could be some here tonight. Though I didn't want any of it. I wasn't a drinker at all, and being this close to water? I didn't want to lose control.

"What are you talking about?" I asked warily, noticing how Kyle's lips shone with alcohol after he took a sip. He caught me staring and sent me a knowing smirk.

Blushing, I looked away.

"That guy. Fozzie's nephew," Presley said, her voice dropping an octave as she delivered that particular piece of juicy gossip. "You were talking to him out on the beach."

Oh God. They saw that?

"He was actually touching you," Presley continued, sounding the slightest bit…jealous? No way. "Why?"

Nerves buzzed in my stomach as everyone seemed to go quiet, all attention on me. Biting my lower lip, unable to look in Kyle's direction, I said hesitantly, "I ran into him."

"Okay," Presley said slowly when I remained quiet. "And then?"

"He grabbed hold of me to make sure I wasn't going to fall." I took another deep breath, struggling to keep my voice steady. "Then he told me I shouldn't be out here and he was going to write me up."

"What an asshole," Presley said, her big blue eyes wide.

"I know, right?" Everyone laughed and I smiled, the nerves settling somewhat. "I told him he couldn't tell me what to do and came over here."

"You did *not*," Presley breathed, her gaze turning admiring. "So ballsy."

"Very ballsy for a new girl," Kyle drawled. He held the flask out toward me. "You should take a drink."

"Um…" How to say no without looking like a total loser?

"There's hardly any left." Presley snatched the flask from his fingers and brought it to her lips. "I'm impressed, though, Annie. Next time I'll make sure to bring enough to share with you."

"Okay. Good." I nodded, thankful I wouldn't have to drink. The only time I'd ever had alcohol was a glass of champagne at my cousin Lydia's wedding.

"Selfish," Kyle muttered, shaking his head. "Our new girl had a traumatic experience with Jake the snake tonight. She needs something to calm her nerves."

"Ew, did you really just call him Jake the snake?" Presley laughed. "You're the snake, Kyle."

"Am not," he said, sounding like a sullen ten-year-old boy.

"He was kind of mean," I added. Kelsey's arm was still looped through mine, and she gave it a squeeze. "He looked… really angry." And intense. So intense.

"Whatever." Presley grinned and handed the flask back to Kyle. Guess there was more in there than she thought. "He's hot, so I'd forgive him for being mean."

"Is that all you care about, Pres?" Kyle asked, laughing before he took another drink. "Is if a guy is hot or not?"

"Pretty much," she said, which only made Kyle laugh harder.

I laughed along with them, though it felt forced. And I couldn't stop glancing around, the realization that I was standing out on a rickety old dock over deep water making me nervous. So many things could happen that were completely out of my control. We could be caught and get in trouble. The dock could collapse under our extra weight and we could fall into the water. Oh, and then I could drown and die.

Totally overdramatic, but I couldn't shake those thoughts.

"Hey, we should play truth or dare," Kaycee suggested, earning cheers from everyone on that stupid old dock but me.

"And Annie should be up first!" Presley said, sending me a sugary smile that was backed with a hint of venom.

Unease slipped down my spine, and Kelsey stepped forward, her voice clear as she said, "I'll take a dare first."

"Sure you don't want to answer a *very* personal question?" Presley asked.

Kelsey shook her head. "Dare, please."

"I dare you to run to the end of the dock and back with no shirt on," Kyle said, his voice smug.

"Deal." Kelsey smiled, tore her shirt off, and ran down the dock, her shoes slapping against the wood with every step, making the structure rattle. I wanted to hold on to something, anything, but I couldn't. I just had to count on the stupid wood to withstand all of our weight.

Though I wanted nothing more than to follow Kelsey right off that dock and keep running until we were back at the cabin.

"You didn't do what I dared you to," Kyle said when Kelsey returned, out of breath and red-faced.

"I sure did," she said with a smile. "I ran down the dock and back without my shirt on."

"But you have a bikini top on underneath it," Kyle said, waving a hand at her.

"You never said anything about taking that off." She started to laugh when she saw the irritation on his face.

He turned toward me, his dark brows lowered, his mouth set in a thin line. "Your turn. Truth or dare?" he asked, sounding downright hostile. Nothing like my usual dreamy Kyle hellos or what's ups. I could only blame the alcohol he'd been drinking.

"Um, truth?" I didn't have much to hide, and I definitely didn't want to take a dare.

"If you could kiss any boy at camp, who would it be?" Presley stepped forward after asking the question, her smile so smug I wanted to smack it off her face.

"Oh." I laughed, trying to play it off. Desperate to play it off. Kyle was in the forefront of my mind, and so was the hot counselor, not that I could mention either of them.

But all my new friends just stared at me, even Kelsey, waiting for my answer. Most of them were smiling, but not in sympathy. No, they were waiting for me to humiliate myself.

And that hurt more than they could ever know.

"If you don't want to say, you could take a dare," Kyle offered, his voice soft, his gaze meeting mine.

Mesmerized by his eyes, his face, by his mere nearness, I agreed before he could take the offer back.

"Please, I'll take the dare." It couldn't be any worse than that question I so did *not* want to answer.

"I dare you to jump off the dock's ledge and into the water," Kyle said.

Oh wait.

It just got much worse.

# Chapter Six

ANNIE

"I can do this," I whispered under my breath, curling my toes over the rough wood as I teetered on the edge of the dock. The cool wind rushed through the trees. I could hear them rustle in the near distance, felt the breeze wash over my already chilled-from-nerves skin, and I lifted my arms above my head. A pose I'd practiced maybe a handful of times forever ago, since I'd always firmly believed swimming, let alone diving, wasn't for me.

But I was feeling brave tonight. Maybe a little reckless.

Okay, maybe a lot stupid, too.

*Here goes nothing.*

"You can do it, Annie, I know you can," Kelsey whispered just before Presley started her countdown. I couldn't believe I'd agreed to this. But I didn't want to look like a baby in front of Kyle, in front of *any* of them, really. I'd wanted to conquer my greatest fear this summer, but not this early into the season.

Clearly I'd completely lost my mind. At least I had Kelsey keeping the faith.

"One!" Presley whisper-shouted the number from where she stood behind me. I could hear everyone crowding around, a few murmured words, one yelp when one of the guys stepped on Kaycee's toes.

I stood up straighter, stiffening my arms into what I hoped was a perfect arc.

"Two!" We didn't want to get caught, so Presley counted down in a whisper. I really hoped one of these people was a decent swimmer so they could jump in after me and save me if need be.

Well, I hoped one of them would try to save me. My knees knocked against each other in that age-old way they used to do when I was little, and I stiffened my legs, willing them to behave.

"You really want to do this, Annie?" Kelsey's nerves bled through her voice, and I closed my eyes for a brief moment, willing myself to stay strong.

Glancing at her over my shoulder, I sent her a look. One that said, *really? You're asking me this now?*

"Okay, okay. You've got this." She nodded, her smile bright in the silvery light of the half moon.

"Three!" Presley shouted, hopping up and down.

I didn't expect her to say three so fast. I whipped my head around and stared at the lake, the way the gentle waves looked like they were topped with sparkling crystals. The moon's soft glow cast everything in this ethereal sheen that made me think of a fairy tale.

A fairy tale where I suddenly became a flailing, screaming princess who fell off the dock and into the lake in a not-so-graceful leap.

The cold water embraced me, pulling me down, my lungs already burning, and I'd only been under for a few seconds.

*Don't panic, don't panic.*

The words rang in my head as my feet brushed the muddy, gooey bottom—*how deep did I fall, jeez*—and I kicked my legs out as hard as I could, aiming for the top of the water. I opened my eyes but I could see nothing but darkness. Not even the light of the moon could penetrate the murky water, and I spread my arms out, trying to remember what Kelsey told me about diving underwater. Then I took a breath.

Big mistake.

Water slipped into my mouth and I pressed my lips together, my lungs positively aching. Oh God. I was probably going to die in this lake. Barely into my summer camp experience and I was a total goner. I'd never get a chance to flirt with Kyle wearing my favorite bikini. I'd never get the chance to kiss him—or *anyone* for that matter. Heck, I wouldn't even get to experience Dane giving me mouth-to-mouth because he wasn't here. He was in his cabin sleeping, like I should've been.

Pushing aside the negative thoughts, I told myself to get a grip.

It felt like the water was pressing on my chest, and I struggled against it. Imagining I was a rocket shooting through space, pushing upward, high in the sky. Up was my goal, air was my goal, the dock was the ultimate goal, and I closed my eyes, told myself, *I can do it. I can do it.*

*Oh God, I don't think I can do it.*

They say when you're about to die, your life flashes before your eyes in a sequence of events, from the time you were born to the here and now.

But I saw none of that. Just the murky water and Presley's smug face and Kyle staring at me like he couldn't believe I'd jumped off the dock.

*I showed him*, I thought. *I showed all of them.*

And now I was going to die. Just like that time when I was

four. I'd almost died then, but I guess my moment was now.

I sank down, down, down. Giving in. Giving up. I couldn't breathe. I couldn't hardly move, but then I felt arms wrap around me.

Strong, well-muscled arms.

They tugged me upward with little effort, and my body became weak as I slumped against an equally well-muscled chest. My head broke through the water and I took a deep, painful breath, coughing up water as I floated on my back, my savior loosening his grip on me but not ever letting me go.

I clung to him, curling my arm around his, breathing hard as I pressed my fingers into his skin. He was real, solid and warm, and for the briefest, craziest moment I thought it was Kyle who saved me.

But it wasn't.

"You okay?" My hero's deep voice sounded right by my ear and I shivered. Between coughs, I nodded, and his arm tightened around me once more as he pulled me along with him, closer to the dock.

"Oh my God, is she all right?" I heard Kelsey shriek from her perch on the dock. My ears were plugged, every sound muffled like I was still under water, and it was weird. Whoever was dragging me along with him answered with a gruff yes and then, finally, my feet were touching actual ground.

I found my footing, the water lapping against my waist, and I glanced to my left, my newfound hero standing beside me, though he was looking in the opposite direction. For a fleeting moment as I stared at his chest, I thought it might be Dewey, the lifeguard from the pool. Rescuing dumb me from a midnight dare jumping into the lake sounded like something he might do, but I realized quickly that this guy was much more muscular than poor gangly Dewey. Then I even thought it could be Dane, but there'd been no Australian accent. And he wasn't as tall as Dane.

The moment I tilted my head back and saw his face, recognition dawned. It was Jacob. The jerk who told me he was going to write me up for sneaking out with everyone else.

Great. The rudest boy at camp just so happened to save my life. I hoped he wasn't one of those types who expected me to be indebted to him for the rest of the summer or whatever.

I looked away and coughed, water filling my mouth so I had no choice but to avert my head and spit it out. My cheeks felt hot, and I couldn't believe I was embarrassed, but old habits died hard, I guess.

He said nothing, just grabbed my hand and walked/dragged me the rest of the way out of the water, until we were standing on the sandy beach. I heard feet thumping on the dock and I glanced up, watched in disbelief as the majority of my so-called friends and the boys from B7B ran off the dock. Not a one of them had stayed behind to see if I was okay.

Not a single one of them.

Were they scared they'd get in trouble? Would Jacob rat me out? He was the director's nephew, after all. I needed to say something to him. I didn't want to get in trouble. I didn't want to be sent home, and I'm pretty sure he had the power to make both things happen.

Before I could say anything, though, Jacob grabbed my shoulders and gave them a little shake so I'd look up at him. His eyes were dark, his mouth set in a grim line, and he bent his knees a little so our gazes were even. "You really all right?" he asked, his tone firm.

I'd quit coughing, but my voice still came out slightly wheezy. "I'm fine." My bones felt like jelly and I thought I might pass out from lack of oxygen, but yeah. I was great.

He squeezed my bare shoulders with his big hands, his fingers sliding over my thin bikini straps, and I realized I'd never stood this close to a boy before with so little clothing on. A shiver moved through me, and I tried to take a step back for much-needed distance, but he wouldn't let me go.

"That was really stupid, jumping off the dock like that," he said, his deep voice now full of irritation.

"Trust me, I wasn't trying to impress you." I couldn't believe I'd said that. But I was offended that he basically just called me stupid.

"No kidding." He released his hold on my shoulders and walked a few steps away, snatching up something off the beach. "And I definitely wasn't impressed."

I made an incredulous sound, one I usually saved for the privacy of my bedroom when no one else was around, and he sent me a look. I was reluctant to admit it was sort of a cute look, his dark eyebrows raised, as if he dared me to contradict him.

So I did.

"Are you going to write me up?" When he still said nothing, I continued. "You said you would earlier." I glanced around, noticed that the dock was completely empty.

Where was Kelsey, anyway? Did she leave me, too?

"You want me to?"

"N-no. O-of c-course n-not." My teeth had started to chatter. I didn't know if it was from the cold or the shock, or a combination of both, but I couldn't make them stop.

"Did you bring a towel with you at least?" Jacob asked. When I shook my head, he muttered something that sounded distinctly like a curse word starting with the letter *F*. The sympathetic look he shot my way was surprising as he came back toward me, his hand thrust outward, a ball of fabric clutched in it. "Take this."

I didn't want him feeling sorry for me. And that didn't look like a towel. "Wh-what i-is it?" I wrapped my arms around my middle, my fingers brushing against my goose-bump-covered torso. I couldn't stop shaking. It was like I had no control over my body.

He sighed and glanced to his left, then his right, like he wanted to make sure there was no one around before he stepped forward and stretched the dark fabric between his hands. "Don't move," he ordered, his tone bossy as he yanked the fabric over my head.

I jerked against his first touch, but otherwise I remained still. It was a giant hoodie that he slipped over my head. Warm and soft and a little sandy from when he'd abandoned it on the beach. The fabric clung to my damp skin and the hem fell to my thighs, covering me from my neck to almost my knees. I shoved my arms in the sleeves but they were so long, they swallowed my hands completely, even when I stretched my fingers out.

He stepped closer and reached behind my head, pulling the hood up so that it covered my soaked hair. Then he grabbed hold of the strings at the sweatshirt's neck and tugged on them, so the hood cinched around my face tightly, his gaze never leaving mine. "Better?"

I nodded and took a deep breath, the shivering starting to subside, thank goodness. "Much."

Jacob reached out and wiped one cheek, then the other, his thumb rough yet warm against my chilled skin. "You're still wet."

"I should p-probably take a shower." I clamped my freezing lips shut. Why did I just say that? Showers meant naked, and I didn't want to talk about getting naked with *Jacob*. Ugh. Not that I meant it that way.

Why couldn't Kyle have been the one to save me? That would've been my dream come true, my summer plans come to fruition in only a few days' time. I could've swooned and fallen into his arms and he would've realized just how amazing and wonderful I was, all because I almost drowned by trying to prove to myself that I wasn't afraid…

"Jake! Is that you? What's going on?"

Oh God. I wanted to die. Just…collapse into the sand and pray it swallowed me whole. I saw the camp director running toward us, his expression full of concern and slightly…angry?

We were so screwed.

• • •

## JAKE

"Play along," I told the girl who was blinking up at me with terrified eyes. They were big and wide and the deepest blue, though the moon could be playing tricks on me. But her eyes were definitely pretty. "Let me do all the talking."

She squeaked in response and I shoved her behind me, smiling at Uncle Bob like I was always hanging out by the lake at midnight.

"Hey, Uncle Bob." I waved at him when he came to a skidding stop in front of me, wearing pale blue pajama pants and a thin white V-neck T-shirt. Damn, I could see all sorts of hair sprouting out, like it could barely be contained, and I almost wanted to laugh.

Almost.

"What are you doing out here at this time of night?" he demanded.

"Technically it's the morning," I joked, my smile fading when I saw his eyes narrow. Yeah, needed to take this a different route. "I was, uh, walking the grounds."

"With a girl?" Bob asked pointedly.

I played dumb. "What girl?"

"Maybe the one I found on the dock?" He tilted his head. "Or perhaps the one hiding behind you?"

The girl on the dock was probably this girl's friend—the only loyal one she had. I'd heard a blood-curdling scream when I was on the far side of the beach, freaked out that someone must've plunged to their death. I saw the group that had been hanging out on the dock yelling and pointing, a few of them running away. One of them stood by the edge of the dock, a redhead who looked terrified as she pointed out into the water.

"Who'd you find on the dock?" I asked.

"A camper from G7A," Uncle Bob said.

"Ah." I had no idea what to say next. I could practically feel the girl shaking behind me, her teeth lightly chattering. She needed to go take that hot shower she mentioned and climb into bed. Forget this entire night ever happened.

"Who's the girl standing behind you, Jake?" Bob crossed his arms in front of his broad chest, looking like he had all night to listen to my explanation.

Dread filled me but I stood taller, the cool night air rippling over my still-damp naked skin and making me shiver. I'd thrown my hoodie on earlier without a shirt and it was damn cold out here. "Ah, she's…" Crap, I didn't know her name. I didn't know who she was. I knew she had a nice rack that filled out her bikini top to perfection. I knew she was a dumbass for jumping into the lake and that her friends were jerks to not try to save her.

"Um, it's me. Annie." She stepped around me, actually daring to say something when I told her to follow my lead. She was either gutsy or dumb as rocks. "From cabin G7A."

Ah, crap. My uncle was going to put two and two together and think I was up to no good, and he was partially right. My earlier intentions with Lacey had been bad, so thank God I hadn't gone through with it. Saving this girl's life was the actual good part. But I'd probably end up still looking like a jerk *and* pissing off my uncle.

Bob frowned at her, then at me, then back at her again. "What are you doing out here at this time of night? There is a curfew, you know."

"I know. I'm so sorry." She sighed and tilted her head

down, her entire face practically swallowed up by my hoodie. "I was just…missing my parents so much. This is my first time at camp and I was feeling homesick. I thought I'd come out and sit on the dock by the water and then I accidentally…fell in."

I blinked at her, but she didn't even look at me. She was saving her performance for my uncle.

Impressive.

"Well." Uncle Bob's voice was gruff as he scratched at the back of his neck. A sure sign he didn't know how to react. He probably wanted to bust her, but she was saying all the right things. And she took the attention off of me. "Thank goodness Jake was out here, then."

"Yes. He saved my life," Annie said gravely. "I'm sorry, though, that I caused so much trouble." She turned to look at me, her eyes wide and unblinking. "I hope you can forgive me."

"I'm just glad you're okay," I muttered, not sure what else to say. She looked like a good girl, she acted like a good girl, but she could put on a damn good performance.

"Jake, walk this young lady back to her cabin," he demanded before turning his attention to Annie. "Do you need to see the nurse?"

"Oh, no. I'm fine," she said with a nod. "But thank you."

"All right then." He studied us both, his gaze razor sharp, head tilted, like he still wasn't quite sure if he could believe us or not. He pointed at Annie. "I don't want to see you out here this late at night ever again, young lady."

"You won't," she said solemnly. "I promise."

Uncle Bob made a harrumphing noise before he turned and headed back to his cabin. We watched him go, us standing next to each other, until he disappeared out of sight.

I finally turned to look at her. "Ready to go?"

She nodded, and we headed toward the girls' cabins. "You

don't need to walk me the whole way," she said.

"If you get lost or somehow fall back into the lake and my uncle finds out I wasn't with you? There will be hell to pay," I muttered. "I'll drop you off in front of G7A and watch you walk through the door."

"So Fozzie Bear is really your uncle?" She sounded surprised, though she also sounded like she already knew this. Rumors spread like wildfire around here. The older campers didn't have their phones, so they sat around and gossiped instead.

"Yep," I said grimly, not giving her any more information. Why add fuel to the gossip fire?

"Oh."

We remained silent for a while, walking the path side by side, me kicking a rock off the trail and her sinking her hands into the front pocket of my hoodie. A hoodie I really wished I was wearing because I was freezing my ass off. Felt like the temperature was dropping with every minute that passed. It was worth giving to her though, because she looked pretty cute wearing it.

"I know you told me to follow your lead," she said after a while, her voice low as we started to pass the cabins. "But I thought it would work better if the excuse came from me."

"No, you're right. What you said was—perfect." She totally deflected Bob's attention off of me, and I appreciated it.

"I'm glad I could help." She sent me a sidelong glance. "Your uncle would be mad if he thought we were somehow... messing around or whatever, right?" Her voice squeaked a little when she said the words.

Cute.

"Definitely." I nodded.

"And you...saved my life." She cleared her throat, as if that admission was hard to make. "Thank you for that."

"Anytime." I wasn't going to give her a lecture or make her feel bad. Forget that. When I first dragged her out of the water I had been scared—and mad. What idiot jumped into the lake late at night? Maybe she didn't realize her friends were so shitty, but still. It was a bad move.

But I was over it now. She saved my ass, too, so we were even.

"It was really dumb of me to do that. I had a momentary burst of confidence, I guess, and thought I could pull it off."

"Next time you have one of those bursts of confidence? Make sure it's in the middle of the day, and there's a lifeguard on duty." I nudged her shoulder with mine and she nearly stumbled off the trail. I reached out and grabbed a shirtsleeve, keeping her from tipping over. Shit, I didn't know my own strength or what? "Sorry about that."

She giggled and tugged on the edge of the hood, shoving it off her head so her still-damp, dark blond hair shone in the moonlight. "This night isn't working out as planned."

"Tell me about it." I agreed, which only made her giggle harder.

It was kind of a cute sound. I was never one to think much of giggling girls because most of the time, they were annoying. But this one—she was all right. I guess. Any other chick would've ratted my ass out and I would've ended up in deep trouble. But for some weird reason, Annie had my back.

"I don't know how to swim," she admitted softly.

I stopped and grabbed hold of her arm, turning her so she had to face me. "Are you serious?"

She nodded, her teeth sinking into her lower lip. "Really stupid of me to jump into the lake, right?"

"Uh, yeah." My voice dripped with sarcasm.

"We were playing truth or dare and I took the dare. I was trying to prove to myself that I was brave. That I could do anything if I just set my mind to it." She shrugged, my hoodie flopping all around her. She really was tiny. "I've never been very daring."

"What you did tonight was pretty damn daring."

Her face brightened, and she beamed. Why she took my words as praise I don't know, but I didn't argue with her. "You really think so?"

"Oh, yeah." I nodded.

Her smile faded. "I need someone to teach me how to swim." She hesitated. "Maybe you could help me?"

"Uh, I don't know about that…" Yeah, I was certified and I'd helped Dewey during the first session giving lessons, but always to the younger kids. I was the master of the guppies. That's what the first session kids called me, and I ran with it.

She shifted closer to me, her hands going to my chest. "Please? It would help me out so much. I just…I feel lame, being the only sixteen-year-old in this entire camp who can't swim."

I glanced down to where her hands touched me. Her fingertips felt like they were charged, sending tiny electrical currents shooting all over my skin. It was…strange. "I have a pretty full schedule."

Her hands dropped from my chest, and disappointment crashed through me. "I'll…I'll tell your uncle you were out here with a girl." When I stared at her blankly, she continued. "That you were hooking up with her."

"Wait, what?" I reared back, shocked by her words. Shocked even more that she'd ventured so close to the truth, even though nothing really happened. This chick could totally play hardball.

She curled her arms in front of her chest, her expression fierce. "I saw Lacey approach you after I left. You were meeting up with her, right?"

Well. I couldn't deny that. "Are you serious right now?"

"As a heart attack." She nodded, her expression still

fierce. She wasn't going to back down. "Just…teach me how to swim. I…I dare you."

Why did she dare me? Was she trying to force me to help her? It would probably take the entire month camp was in session or longer to teach her. From what I witnessed, I wouldn't call her the most natural swimmer in the world. No way was I tying myself to this girl for weeks on end teaching her how to doggy-paddle. "I'll give you three lessons."

"Ten."

"Seven."

"Deal." She smiled, dropping her arms to her sides. "There. That wasn't so bad, was it?"

Huh. I had a feeling this could end up being a major mistake.

# Chapter Seven

## ANNIE

I still couldn't believe I'd had the nerve to talk to Jacob like that. Or Jake. Whatever I should call him, the more time we'd spent together last night, the more I realized he was actually really good-looking, with those dark brown eyes and dark, touchable hair—when he wasn't acting so grumpy. And he'd saved my life, sacrificed his hoodie (which smelled really good, like citrusy clean boy), and treated me like I was a regular girl, not some nerd he could barely tolerate.

And he had a really nice chest. Firm and warm and smooth. I mean, I actually *touched* him last night. Gave him grief, dared him to spend more time with me…

Who am I? A week at camp and I've completely transformed myself already? Or am I just getting started?

We were sitting in the dining hall finishing breakfast in our pajamas, and Kelsey had a captive audience, telling everyone my rescue story. I was still wearing Jacob's hoodie. Kelsey wouldn't stop talking about what happened last night.

How Fozzie Bear busted her out on the dock. What a hero Jacob was for running into the lake and saving my drowning butt.

"He literally just tore off that hoodie, tossed it onto the sand, and ran into the water before he smoothly dived under, disappearing like he was some sort of dolphin or something. It was freaking amazing, " Kelsey said for about the hundredth time.

"Yeah, I'm sure," Kaycee said, sounding bored. She looked at Hailey and they both stood, picking up their trays. "We're headed back to the cabin. Who wants to come with?"

Everyone stood but Kelsey and me, and they all left in a flurry of quick movement, talking about plans for the day. I watched them go, thinking I should've gone with them, but the minute they walked away, Kelsey started griping.

"They didn't even really say sorry." She looked disgusted. "You took their dare and nearly died, yet they act like it's no big deal."

"Technically it was Kyle who made the dare," I pointed out, earning a glare from Kelsey.

"That doesn't make it any better. He should apologize, too. They all should." Kelsey shook her head, grabbing her orange juice and taking a drink. "I still feel bad that I couldn't help you. I tried."

"I know you did." Fozzie Bear sent her back to the cabin, so there was nothing she could do. I wasn't mad at her. I wasn't mad at anyone, really. Just mostly irritated with myself for doing something so stupid.

"Well, I'm sorry. I feel like I should apologize again."

I nibbled on a bagel, my gaze scanning the room, trying to ignore the disappointment that filled me when I couldn't find Kyle yet again. He hadn't come with his cabin group, which was weird. "You don't have to. I know you're really sorry."

"Oh. Right." The disappointment in my new friend's

voice was clear. "Well, at least you had Jake to save you. Seriously, why aren't you completely dazzled by his heroic performance? He saved your freaking *life*, Annie. And it was the coolest thing ever," Kelsey stressed.

"Uh-huh." I couldn't focus on what Kelsey said. I was too busy looking for Kyle.

"He's really good-looking, too, you know. In that dark, brooding way," Kelsey added.

For a moment I wanted to correct her. Kyle wasn't dark and brooding...

But then I realized she was still talking about Jacob. I remembered the deep timbre of his voice when he'd asked if I was all right. The selfless way he tugged his sweatshirt over my head, how he wiped the water from my cheeks, his touch gentle.

What he looked like, his hair wet and his lips parted as he stood in front of me.

I shifted on the bench, hating the weird, tingly sensation that swept over me at the memory.

He chose that moment to shuffle into the dining hall, accompanied by none other than my crush, Kyle. Dreamy, sleep-rumpled Kyle, who wore a faded black T-shirt with holes around the neck and hem and obnoxious pajama bottoms emblazoned with the Atlanta Falcons emblem all over them.

They were awful. I hated the Falcons only because my dad did, too. But I could forgive Kyle for the mistake. His cuteness more than made up for his bad taste in football.

"Oh, it's Prince Dreamy and your swim coach right now," Kelsey said amusedly, nudging me in the ribs. I should've never told her about the swim lessons thing. "Who knew they were friends?"

I dropped my bagel, and it landed on my plate with a loud *plop*, the crumbs bouncing, my gaze locked on Kyle and... fine, on Jacob. They had all the girls' attention in the dining hall, really. Like a symphony of sighs went up at the same time at the sight of two sleepy, hot boys striding into the room like they owned the place.

Wait a minute. Did I just put Jacob under the hot category? He was good-looking but sort of a jerk. And his attitude should've canceled out his looks.

But he *did* save me. I needed to focus on the positives. The fact that he was going to teach me how to swim so I wouldn't be a total embarrassment and could hang out at the lake with Kyle and everyone else like a normal person. I needed Jacob right now, and I couldn't forget that.

"What time is your lesson?" Kelsey asked.

"Huh?" I turned to look at her, saw the knowing expression on her face, and immediately felt dumb. "I don't know. We didn't discuss times."

"Hmm, well, don't you think now is the perfect opportunity to go talk schedules and lessons?" Kelsey waggled her brows, making me laugh.

Making me nervous.

"I can't go talk to him now. They're still in line."

"So? Wait a few minutes and once they sit down, then go over and talk to him. Then you can talk to Kyle, too, and get his attention. Maybe he'd apologize, you know? He should." Kelsey smiled, though it felt reluctant. "It's a win-win for you, see?"

She was right, I supposed. But she was also banking on my being way braver than I really was. Just because I jumped off the dock last night and almost killed myself didn't mean I was brave. No, last night's incident just meant I was stupid.

"Sure," I said, sounding much more confident than I felt. "Sounds perfect."

Kelsey chugged her orange juice, then gazed longingly at my bagel. "You gonna finish that?"

I shook my head, and she snatched it from the plate,

downing it in two bites. For such a string bean she sure could put the food down. No way could I eat like that and be as thin as Kelsey. Though she seemed just as self-conscious as I was about showing her body in a swimsuit.

That had been hard, tugging off my shirt and stepping out of my shorts last night wearing the two-piece in front of everyone, though they hadn't paid me much attention. Not even Kyle. Though I remembered the way Jacob looked at me last night, once he dragged me up to shore. His gaze had almost seemed appreciative.

And he would see me in my bikini again today, when he gave me my first lesson. Would I get that same appreciative look? Or would he keep me at a distance, playing stern instructor to dopey new student? And where would he give me these lessons, at the lake? That was where he worked lifeguard duty…

Panic rose within me and I took a deep breath, trying to fight it. Why didn't I think of that? People were going to see Jacob and me today, if he planned on giving me that lesson at the lake, which wouldn't work. No way. I didn't think this through. I couldn't be seen with Jake. What if it got back to Kyle? Plus, then they would all know I couldn't swim for crap and I would look like a total loser. I don't want to give them more reasons to laugh at me.

We should've arranged for private lessons. Night lessons. Though I think he'd rather spend his nights doing anything else but teach me how to freaking swim…

"Hey, Annie."

That drawl was unmistakable. Could I maybe close my eyes and I'd disappear so he wouldn't notice me sitting here?

Kelsey's sharp elbow in my ribs—again—told me no.

"Um, hi." I lifted my gaze to Jacob's, saw that he clutched a tray overloaded with food in his hands. Kyle stood next to him, his tray equally full, a curious expression on his face as his gaze went from Jacob to me.

"Mind if we sit here?" Jacob asked, waving at the empty spot across from us.

Kelsey's jaw just about dropped to the floor. "Um, aren't you supposed to sit with your cabin?" She looked directly at Kyle while I tried my hardest not to blush, but it was no use. My cheeks felt like they were on fire.

"My group's gone," Kyle said as he and Jacob sat down, Jacob directly across from me while Kyle sat across from Kelsey. Both boys dug in without saying a word, and I cataloged everything on Jacob's tray.

A banana, an apple, a blueberry muffin, scrambled eggs and bacon, strawberry yogurt, an orange juice, and a chocolate milk. Oh, wait, make that *two* blueberry muffins. He already had one halfway stuffed into his mouth.

"You boys sure do eat a lot," Kelsey said, laughing.

Jacob smiled, his mouth curved and lips sealed, thank goodness. I did not want to see chewed-up muffin in his mouth. "You're the girl from the dock," he said to her after he swallowed.

Kelsey nodded, looking pleased. "Kelsey."

"Jake." He flicked his head in Kyle's direction. "This is Kyle. And that's Annie. Though I think you two already know each other." He pointed at me, his gaze dropping, taking in the fact that I was wearing his hoodie, no doubt.

Busted.

"Yeah." Kyle wasn't overly friendly this morning. He just grunted his hello before taking a big bite of banana.

"Kyle's not much of a morning person," Jake said, holding up his hand at the side of his mouth, like he was telling us a great secret.

"Neither is Annie," Kelsey said, earning a dirty look for her totally unnecessary comment. Why did she have to bring up my faults? Though I guess it gave Kyle and me something in common, so that was a good thing, right?

"Hmm, I bet, especially this morning." The knowing look in Jacob's eyes made me want to kick him.

• • •

## JAKE

She was so incredibly easy to get a rise out of. I sat with Annie and her friend just to bug her. I ran across Kyle in front of the dining hall just as I was about to go in. He was running late, since he slept in and didn't come with the rest of his cabin group, which was weird. But Brian was his counselor, and he cut everyone slack—which would totally piss off Uncle Bob.

But what Uncle Bob didn't know couldn't hurt him.

I warned Kyle as we entered the dining hall that I didn't want to sit near Lacey, considering she was the first person I saw. Girl tried to talk to me last night when I went back to the staff cabins—I found her waiting for me outside, pacing back and forth. When I told her I had nothing more to say to her, she started to yell, calling me all sorts of names and even waking up Dane and Nancy.

The girl was nuts.

I'd walked into the dining hall with my breath held and my guard up, but she hadn't looked in my direction. Thank God.

"So. You're Dane's assistant. Right?" Kelsey pushed aside her plate and leaned forward, her elbow on the table, her chin propped on her curled fist. She had that dreamy look in her eyes like all the girls did when they talked about lame-ass Dane. "What's it like, working for him?"

Could I tell her he was an egotistical prick? That would be a lie, but still. It would be fun to create a new rumor about my so-called boss. The guy wasn't that bad, but he did think he was God's gift to women, and the way all the girls chased after him while they wiped the drool from their mouths, it proved he sort of was. Not that he touched any of those girls. He wouldn't dare, and he wasn't stupid. He was way too old for them. Plus, he had a girlfriend in Australia he called all the damn time. She hated his summer camp job because it kept them apart.

I was pretty sure he loved it because every summer, he was king of the lake with his adoring harem surrounding him.

"He's cool," I said as noncommittally as I could. I tried my best not to talk about Dane. I'd realized quickly that he preferred the mystique surrounding him, so I helped support it.

"He's more than cool, and you know it." Kelsey sighed and smiled. "I think it's his accent. He always sounds so sexy, even saying the most boring thing ever. I could listen to him talk all day long." She sat up straighter, her hand falling to the table. "I bet I'd die if I went to Australia and had to listen to those accents all day long. Just straight up keel over."

Hmm. Kelsey was sort of dramatic.

My gaze slid to Annie, who was staring blatantly at Kyle as he wolfed down his breakfast. "What about you?" I asked her, but she wasn't listening.

She started when Kelsey poked her in the shoulder. "What?" she asked her friend.

Kelsey pointed at me, and Annie's gaze met mine. "Um, did you ask me something?" She sounded nervous.

"Yeah. I wanted to know if you have a crush on Dane, too? Like your friend."

Kelsey laughed. "I don't have a crush on him."

"Oh! No." Annie shook her head, her cheeks going beet red. She blushed a lot. It was kind of cute. "I mean, he's hot and all but..." Her gaze slid to Kyle again, like she couldn't help herself. Kyle didn't even notice. He just kept chewing with his mouth open, then burped. Annie didn't even flinch.

"He's not really my type."

Bells started dinging in my head. I think I might've figured out who her type was.

Interesting.

And just the slightest bit…disappointing?

"Oh, like you'd have a chance with him, even if he was your type," Kelsey said, laughing. "He has too many to choose from, considering every girl here talks about him like he's the hottest guy at camp."

"That's because he *is* the hottest guy at camp," Kyle said, suddenly finding his voice. The girls both turned their rapt attention to him, their eyes wide, and he leaned back, making a face. "What? It's true."

"Seriously, dude?" That's all I bothered to say.

"You think Dane is hot?" Kelsey asked, trying her best to keep a straight face. "Are you president of his fan club?"

"No, dummy. Dane doesn't have a fan club. At least, if he does, I've never heard about it." Holy shit, sometimes Kyle was as dumb as a box of rocks. "We just know all the girls lose their shit every time he so much as walks by, let alone when he talks to one of them. It's pretty damn obvious. No one bothers to hide it." His response was greeted with dead silence. Even I'm surprised he'd have so much to say about Dane the lifeguard stud.

When no one said anything, Kyle rolled his eyes and started peeling back the wrapper on his blueberry muffin. "I'm going to quit talking now."

"You do that," I said, clapping him on the back, smiling at both Kelsey and Annie. But they weren't even looking in my direction. They were too busy whispering to each other behind their cupped hands.

I hated when girls did that. Made me nervous, like they were talking about me, which they probably were. Kyle was oblivious, too busy stuffing his face, and I tried to follow his lead, concentrating on shoving as much food in my stomach before I was out for the long haul at the lake. I rarely got a break until lunch, and usually by then I was starving.

We made small talk for the next few minutes. And when I refer to "we" I should clarify that it was Kelsey who did all the talking. Kyle and I ate. Annie watched Kyle eat as discreetly as possible.

Meaning, she wasn't very discreet at all. What with the wide eyes and the rosy cheeks, it was fairly obvious that she was crushing on Kyle hard. Though he was the only one who didn't seem to notice.

"Gotta go hit the showers," Kyle announced as he sprang up from the bench and grabbed his now-empty tray. "See you at the lake," he told me before he walked away.

He didn't even acknowledge the girls' existence with a good-bye.

"So tell me the truth," I said the moment Kyle was out of earshot. "You have a thing for Kyle."

"Oh, I don't like him at all." Kelsey rested her hand on her chest like she was shocked by what I said. "That would be An—"

Annie clamped her hand over her friend's mouth, muffling whatever else she was about to say. "Don't listen to her. She has no idea what she's talking about." The glare Annie sent her friend was murderous.

"It's okay if you like the guy." I leaned across the table, my smile easy, my mind trying to come up with something that I could blackmail her with right back. I think I just found it. "I'm sure he'd love to know *all* the juicy details."

She turned her murderous glare on me. Was it okay to admit that I thought she was kind of hot with the furious expression, lack of makeup, and messy blond bun on top of her head? Upon first glance she looked as harmless as a fluffy kitten.

But those eyes...yeah. They were seriously pissed.

Seriously pretty.

And I had no business thinking like that. Campers were off-limits.

"Hey Kels, would you be a dear and leave Jacob and me alone for a few minutes?" Annie asked sweetly, all fluffy kitten-like.

"Um. Sure." Kelsey made her escape in seconds. I think angry Annie scared the crap out of her.

The moment we were alone, Annie's smile faded and she parted her lips, ready to attack, but I spoke first.

"You don't have to call me Jacob."

Her lips snapped back together. "Huh?"

"You called me Jacob. You keep calling me Jacob."

"Isn't that your name?"

"Well, yeah." I shrugged. "But everyone calls me Jake."

"Oookay." She dragged the word out, then shook her head, making a little face. "That's not the point. The point is I need you to never, *ever* repeat anything about me having a crush on Kyle to anyone." She paused. "Especially Kyle."

I said nothing. Just peeled back the foil seal on my yogurt and dunked a plastic spoon in it, stirring it around.

"It's not even true, that I have a crush on him." Her voice shook a little. Meaning she was probably lying. "We've only been here barely a week. Not like I know him or anything."

"That's how crushes normally start," I said conversationally, keeping my cool. Not even looking at her. I bet it was driving her nuts. "You see someone, think they're hot, next thing you know, you've got a crush." I scooped up the yogurt and took a bite, then made a face. It tasted like strawberry-flavored goo. If I were alone I'd spit it out, but I didn't want to gross Annie out, so I reluctantly swallowed the shit down. Man, that was gross.

"Yeah, well, that's not how mine started. I mean—I

don't even have a crush on him, so nothing started. No crush, nothing to talk about. Nothing to see here!" The last line I figured was a joke, but she wasn't laughing, and neither was I.

I chanced a glance at her and saw her cheeks were bright red as usual, and the worry shining in her eyes was obvious. I should just put this girl out of her misery and let her off the hook.

But I'm sort of an asshole, and I enjoyed seeing her squirm. Just a little bit. So I remained silent.

When I still hadn't said anything, she leaned across the table, the neck of her tank top slipping and offering me a glimpse of her—bright pink bra? *Nice.*

"It's okay. I swear I won't tell anyone."

She sat up straighter, her lips curving into a pretty smile. "Thank—"

"Though I don't know why you're so worried about anyone finding out. From what I've heard, he's been with pretty much every girl in your cabin," I added.

The pretty smile fell, her eyes going dim. "Trust me, I know," she mumbled, her disappointment visible.

I sort of hated that she was disappointed. And I was the one who disappointed her, even though it was with information regarding the tool, aka Kyle. Not like I did anything to her personally. "So I'd guess you have a solid chance with the guy."

"I so don't want to have this conversation right now, especially with you."

Ouch. Whatever. "I get it." I stood, my gaze locked on hers. "Just…don't be so down on yourself when it comes to Kyle."

She frowned. "Why do you say that?"

"Because maybe you have more to offer him than he deserves."

Her eyes went wide and her mouth popped open. "What

do you mean?" she asked, her voice soft, her head tilted to the side like what I just said confused the hell out of her.

But I didn't answer.

I was already gone. Hightailing my ass out of there before I said something really stupid. Like that she was cute and she seemed smart and she could do so much better than Kyle. Not that I really knew her. Not that I knew anything about her. It was just a sense I had. She was definitely better than the tool.

She was probably better than me, too.

# Chapter Eight

## JAKE

After leaving Annie behind, I felt like a world-class jerk.

Know how when you're in a crowded place and you see someone? Maybe even make eye contact with them and talk for a little while? Afterward, every time you walk around that same crowded place, you see them. Again. And again. Until it becomes this strange coincidence that doesn't feel like a coincidence at all.

More like it was meant to be.

That was happening with Annie. Everywhere I looked, there she was. I stopped by to deliver boxes at the arts and crafts building, and boom, there was Annie sitting at a table, making a lanyard. I passed a cluster of trees not too far from the dining hall and there she was, sitting next to Kelsey, staring at me with hurt and confusion filling her eyes.

I looked away, feeling like an ass.

Afternoon activities were usually total chaos, so Dane and I always manned the lake. I sat in the lifeguard tower while Dane was on the ground, making sure everyone was properly using their paddles while in the canoes or kayaks and not smacking the crap out of each other. The younger boys loved nothing more than splashing the girls with their paddles until they were soaked, which always caused lots of screeching and out-of-control behavior.

Meaning one of us almost always had to be on canoe duty.

I'm sitting in the chair under the shade that kept the sun off me so I wouldn't burn to a crisp, my sunglasses on, a whistle on a cord around my neck. Some of the older girls liked to mill around on the tiny beach near the lifeguard post, flashing one of us—usually Dane—flirtatious smiles and cleavage shots. I didn't get as much potential boob action as Dane did, but I'd had my fair share. Pretty distracting when I'm supposed to be watching the water, but we really had no swimmers who would go too far out, so I was mostly in the clear.

I leaned forward and propped my elbows on my thighs, my gaze sharp as I scanned the lake. Some of the canoes were out now, and they were keeping the rowdy play to a minimum. Dane was still on the shore, helping load up the kayaks with kids, blowing his whistle every ten seconds to get the campers to pay attention to whatever he was saying. The weather was extra hot today, so it seemed everyone chose a water sport as their afternoon activity.

Never been more thankful to not have to work the ground. Usually lifeguard tower detail was boring. No one was drowning out here.

Except possibly Annie.

I knew she wasn't at the lake, since I hadn't seen her. Not that I was really looking, but I figured she'd just pop up anyway. I grabbed the binoculars and once more scanned the area, totally not looking for Annie. I moved beyond the lake, checking out the rest of the grounds.

Yep, there she was. Sitting in front of the arts and crafts

building on a bright pink beach towel, talking with the group of girls from her cabin. They were all chatting animatedly, I could tell even from this distance, and I knew that most of the girls in G7A were one-half of the popular clique that lorded over the camp like a bunch of queen bees.

They were awful.

Lacey was the cabin counselor for G7B and those girls were even worse—just like Lacey. She was the ultimate queen bee, yet I'd had no problem hanging out with her.

What sort of guy did that make me?

A guy who learned his lesson and now wanted to steer clear, that's who.

Tearing my gaze away from Annie and her little group of friends, I did another scan of the lake. The boys were splashing the girls with their paddles, but it was harmless stuff. The kayaks were headed out, one at a time, Dane yelling commands and blowing his whistle like a crazy man.

Shit. This was really boring.

I grabbed my baseball cap and slipped it on backward, setting the binoculars to the side before I leaned back in my chair, grabbing the book I'd brought with me. Not that I'm a secret reader or anything, but what else was I going to do while I sat up here for two hours and Dane has everything under control on the ground?

At least it was a gorgeous day. The sky was this bright, almost fake-looking blue, dotted with puffy white clouds. The slightest breeze would waft past not often enough, swaying the big pines that surrounded the camp and rattling the leaves in the poplar trees that were everywhere.

I'd never been up here in the fall, but I'd bet it looked pretty damn magical. Not that I was a big fan of fall leaves or anything. Seriously, who cared about that shit? They all just eventually fell off, only to sprout back up again. The circle of life and all that crap.

I'm like the Lion King over here.

"You're a moron."

I glanced down to see Kyle standing at the base of the lifeguard tower, classic Ray-Bans covering his eyes and wearing the ugliest, brightest Hawaiian-print swim trunks I'd ever seen. I stashed my book so he wouldn't see it, wishing I didn't care if he did.

"Thanks. Nice shorts." I flicked my chin at him and he smiled.

"They're fucking awful. Thanks for noticing." Kyle glanced around, like he was making sure no one was nearby before he said, "We're thinking of sneaking off during movie night. Wanna go with us?"

I inwardly groaned. Was this a conspiracy or what? They all wanted me to sneak off. "Where to?"

"Not sure yet. Blake somehow snuck a bottle of peppermint schnapps in his bag." Kyle's brows waggled above his sunglasses. "Contraband, baby."

"Peppermint schnapps?" If someone were to smuggle in booze to camp, that was the worst crap you could bring. "That stuff is awful."

Kyle shrugged. "It's all we got. Take it or leave it."

I'd rather leave it, but I didn't want to say yes or no yet. What if…Annie would be there? I couldn't imagine her wanting to drink smuggled-in schnapps, but maybe she would. "Where are you guys meeting?"

"We'll talk at movie night. I'll have more details then." He grinned, looking pleased with himself. "Catch ya later."

I watched him go, then slumped against my seat again, wishing he'd stay longer. Talking to a tool was better than having no one to talk to at all. I looked over at my book, but I wasn't in the mood to read. I crossed my arms in front of my chest, which was damp from sweat and my sunscreen melting off. I needed to coat myself with some more soon.

My eyelids felt heavy, and I startled when my head fell forward, then jerked back. Crap, I was falling asleep. I grabbed my water bottle and took a swig. Stood on the tiny platform in front of the chair and stretched my arms above my head. Hating how wobbly this thing was when all I did was stand.

I was tired. Last night's adventures didn't allow for much sleep, especially since my mind had been full of thoughts of Annie, and I could really go for some right now. But I knew that wasn't happening.

No way, no how.

· · ·

## ANNIE

"You should go talk to him," Kelsey said as we sat on the giant pink beach towel and chatted with the other girls from our cabin. They included us in their conversation, but they were clearly talking about something we really didn't have much knowledge about. They didn't bring up last night or Kyle, not even once, thank God.

I was tired of talking about it, so I was fine with that.

"Go talk to who?" I plucked at the grass, pulling it out of the ground one blade at a time. It was thin and sharp, could probably cut my skin if I didn't watch out, but I was feeling reckless. A little hopeless. A lot confused. I didn't know why Jake said those things to me earlier. He didn't give me a chance to ask him, either, taking off without even a good-bye. Every time I saw him around today, which felt like all the time, he'd send me a guilty look before turning away.

I didn't get it. Worse, we never even talked about our swimming lesson plans, which meant I should go find him and ask when we might start. My grand summer camp plans were slipping away from me minute by minute, all because I lacked a certain skill. I would be forever banned to dry land while

Kyle was either in the pool or at the lake. He spent most of his time by the water.

Life was so cruel.

And I was being oh so dramatic.

"Jake!" Kelsey whisper-hissed. She always acted like I should know who or what she was talking about. And when it came to Kelsey, I could never read her mind. "He's working lifeguard duty so no one's really around. Go ask him when he's going to give you those lessons."

"I can't do that." Ugh. If I could slap myself, I so would. That was the old Annie talking. The wimpy, *I can't handle talking to a boy alone* Annie. I swore to myself I wasn't that girl any longer, and I needed to prove it to myself.

"Just flash him your boobs," Kelsey said with a laugh. "Boys love that sort of thing."

She would say that, knowing it was the last thing I'd ever do. "That's a *terrible* idea. I won't flash Jacob—Jake my boobs." I wouldn't flash Kyle my boobs, either. I didn't care if he was my dream crush.

"You act like it's the end of the world, but it's so not. We only just got here! We've barely been here a week! You have *weeks* left to prove to Kyle you're the one for him. All you need are a couple of swim lessons so you can doggy-paddle or whatever. That way you'll feel confident in the water," Kelsey pointed out. We'd sort of turned our backs on the other girls so they weren't listening to our conversation and we weren't listening to theirs.

And I so wished I had Kelsey's confidence that I could make it work with Kyle, but I didn't. She did have a point, though. I could try to convince Jake to teach me a quick doggy paddle and be done with it. I couldn't even manage to do that—doggy-paddle. I'm that bad of a swimmer. I just looked like I was flailing and near death. I'm a hopeless case.

I needed Jake to fix that.

"Just…go over there and show him what God gave you." She checked me out, her eyes roving over me from head to toe, like she was some perverted guy. "You're looking good right now, Annie. Don't waste your time sitting here with us when you could be making conversation with the hotness that is Jacob Fazio."

"Oh my God, keep your voice down," I whispered, reaching out to grab her arm. I didn't want any of the other girls to hear us talking about Jake or Kyle or my stupid plans. And it wasn't Jake I wanted to talk to. It was Kyle.

Kyle, who was headed straight for us—right at this very moment.

I sprang to my feet, ignoring Kelsey, ignoring the other girls as I walked toward him, plastering a smile on my face, trying my best to calm my nerves. I didn't think. I couldn't. Thinking would get me twisted up over the tiny details and that was the last thing I needed.

*Focus. You've got this.*

He wore really ugly board shorts that he somehow could make look good, and he smirked as he stopped directly in front of me, his eyes shaded by sunglasses. I wished I wore some, too, so I could hide behind them. "Hey, new girl," he drawled.

The nickname made me blush, like usual. I seriously hated my fair skin. "Hi, Kyle."

"What are you up to?"

"Nothing much." I shrugged, my brain scrambling to come up with something else. Anything else to keep the conversation going. But the second I got around him, I became tongue-tied. He stole all my words, all my rational thoughts, making me feel useless.

It was weird, how I could talk to Jake so easily yet I became mute around Kyle…

"You going to movie night?" he asked.

"Of course." The girls already warned me movie night was code for covert hookups happening. It was dark, the counselors were lax, Fozzie usually wasn't around. Stolen kisses were on the movie night agenda.

I wondered if Kyle was interested in sitting with me. I wondered if he'd—

"We're sneaking out. Blake's got a secret stash of alcohol." Kyle grinned, looking pleased. "Want to come with?"

My mouth dropped open. Was he seriously asking me to sneak out with him tonight? To go drink alcohol? Why did he keep pushing it on me?

"Sure," I said before I could second-guess myself and say something stupid. Like no.

"Great." He tilted his head to the side, looking at the girls still sitting on the towel, I assumed. "Don't tell your friends, though. Especially that Chelsea girl."

"Her name's Kelsey," I corrected him, though he acted like he didn't hear me. Or didn't care. Probably both. "And why don't you want me to tell them?"

"They have big mouths." He stepped closer and lowered his voice, like he was about to share a big secret. "They'll tell everyone, and we only have one bottle. But for you, new girl? I don't mind sharing with you."

Everything inside me went warm and tingly. He liked me. He must! "Okay," I said softly. "I won't tell."

"Promise?"

I nodded. "I promise."

"Cool. I'll talk to you later. At the movie. We're still in the planning stages." He held out his fist, and I bumped mine against his. Now I felt like his bro or whatever. This guy totally sent mixed signals.

"Sounds good," I said weakly, watching as he gave me a quick wave before he took off.

Kelsey was at my side in seconds. "What did he say?"

"I, um, I think he wants us to sit together tonight," I lied, hoping like crazy she'd believe me.

From the shocked look on her face, I would say she did. "Are you serious? Holy crap, Annie! This is great news!"

"I know." I smiled, glancing over my shoulder to check out Kyle's retreating back. "Crazy, right?"

"Crazy awesome. Now maybe you better go talk to Jake and find out when he's gonna give you that first swim lesson he owes you." Kelsey nudged my shoulder. "Go, my child. Go talk to the other hottest boy in camp."

I glared at her before I headed for the lake, my mind awhirl with all the things. The many, many things that involved all the boys.

Well, two boys, but for me? That may as well be all the boys because hello, at home they never paid attention to me. But at camp? It was almost like I had two of them fighting over me.

More than a slight exaggeration, but still.

As I walked the trail, the white wooden lifeguard tower slowly came into view. I squinted in the sun, lifting my hand up to shield my eyes as I took in dark-haired, golden-skinned Jake sitting there with the whistle between his lips. He wore red swim trunks that looked very lifeguard-official, and sunglasses covered his eyes. With no shirt on and wearing a baseball hat, the breeze rustling the ends of his wavy brown hair this way and that, I'm sure plenty of girls swooned and gasped at the sight of him.

Not me. Not at this particular moment. My mind was full of Kyle. Cute, sweet, always wanting to get me drunk, Kyle.

Okay, that last part wasn't a good quality, but we weren't all perfect, right?

"Good luck! You can do it!" I suddenly heard Kelsey yell from behind me.

Glancing over my shoulder, I glared at my too-hopeful

friend before I huffed out a sigh. I could hear her literally cheering me on, but I refused to look back again.

That would only encourage her.

I gave myself a mental speech as I approached the lifeguard tower. I would keep it short and sweet. Ask him when he wanted to meet and then leave. The best thing would be not to engage. Engaging gave him ammunition, and the guy already had enough on me. I didn't trust him. I didn't necessarily like him, either, even if he did save my life last night.

I stopped just at the base of the tower and glanced up at him. His chin was slumped forward into his neck, toward his chest, and his baseball hat was askew. He wore mirrored sunglasses—and they gave nothing away. "Hey."

No reply.

Taking a deep breath in search of courage, I said, "Jake." It felt sort of weird, calling him Jake. For some reason, I thought of him more as a Jacob. "Can I ask you a question?"

Still no reply. What the heck was wrong with this guy? Was he asleep?

No way.

I stepped forward and wrapped my fingers around the wooden structure, trying to give it a shake, but it was solid as a rock. "Come on, stop ignoring me. It's super annoying," I called up to him.

He said nothing. He didn't even move. I thought I heard a soft snuffing sound—almost like a snore?

He couldn't be.

"Jake!" I yelled his name, not caring if anyone heard me. There was so much noise surrounding us, I doubted anyone was paying me any mind. Looked like Jake wasn't paying anyone any mind, either.

Like no one.

And he was on lifeguard duty. Supposed to be watching

out for the safety of others.

I was fairly certain he was freaking asleep.

The soft snore I heard again confirmed my suspicions.

Deciding the hell with it, I grabbed hold of the slats of the lifeguard tower and climbed up until I was on top, right next to Jake.

Who was still freaking sleeping.

My gaze dropped to the whistle that hung from a thick red cord around his neck. Without thought I reached over and grabbed it, my fingertips grazing the warm, firm skin of his chest. Ignoring the tingles that raced up my arm at that fleeting contact, I wrapped my lips around the whistle.

And blew as hard as I could.

# Chapter Nine

I jumped about a mile when the whistle blowing right in my face startled me awake. Slender fingers wrapped around my arm, trying to steady me, and I sat up straight. Pushing my sunglasses up onto my head, I knocked my baseball cap off so it fell to the ground and I turned, startled to see who was there.

Annie. Sitting next to me on the bench, a smug smile curling her—ah damn, perfect?—lips. She released her hold on me and I scooted away from her as much as I could. I needed the distance, but I wasn't getting it up here on this tiny bench.

"What are you doing here?" I muttered, scrubbing a hand over my face. I blinked hard, my head fuzzy. I didn't remember seeing her approach...

"You were asleep. On the job, when you're supposed to be watching out for all the campers in the lake." Her voice was light and airy, as if she'd just discovered something totally awesome.

Which she sort of did. She discovered something she could totally use against me.

*Shit.*

"What, are you taking over my job?" I sneered, trying to go for mean and surly, but she saw right through me—one of her uncanny abilities. I was really feeling more groggy and half asleep.

"No, but I should. I'm a way better lifeguard than you right about now." She flicked her hair behind her shoulder, still wearing the smug smile.

Despite feeling shitty at being caught freaking sleeping, I couldn't help but think the smug smile was a good look for her.

"Why are you here, Annie?" I asked softly, going for a different tactic. I didn't want to fight with this girl. I didn't want her hating me, either. Why, I didn't know, but I sensed she needed an ally. And I needed one, too. I was tired of spending this summer alone. I hung out with Brian on occasion, but he was mostly too busy trying to hook up with Hannah. And I couldn't hook up with anyone. I couldn't take the risk.

This girl was absolutely, 100 percent off-limits. And... nice. When she wasn't mad at me.

"Um, I was wondering when we could start the swimming lessons." She smiled sweetly, her cheeks turning pink, like they were prone to do. I wondered if her skin was hot to the touch.

I wondered what she might do if I reached out and touched her to see.

"When do you want to start them?"

"I don't know. I was thinking—"

"Watch out!" The Frisbee came out of nowhere, and I grabbed Annie's arm, pulling her close. She ducked her head just as I dodged right, the bright yellow Frisbee flying by us, and I glared at the guilty-looking kid down on the beach. He held his hands up in the air, his friends laughing. "Sorry, man!"

"You all right?" I asked Annie, softening my voice so I didn't sound as hostile as I felt. That Frisbee almost nailed her right in the back of the head. Assholes.

"I-I'm fine," she said shakily, shifting away from me, her eyes wide. "Isn't that the second time you saved me?"

"Guess so." I still hadn't let go of her arm. Her skin was soft and warm. She smelled good. Her hair was wavy, and it blew into her face, irritating her, so she brushed it away again and again. I swore she was wearing eye makeup—her eyes looked a little darker. Why? Did she do it so she could impress Kyle? That jackass wouldn't notice shit.

"Well, thanks." She smiled, looking away from me like she couldn't handle it or something. I don't know. Every time I talked to Annie I was left feeling confused. Like I didn't know what she wanted from me. "I didn't see it coming."

"You wouldn't have, considering it was flying straight toward the back of your head." I smiled and let go of her arm, my fingers sliding across her smooth skin. Little sparks of heat seemed to ignite wherever we made contact, leaving me unsettled.

Yet also wanting…more?

She returned the smile, her cheeks still a little pink, the wind sending her hair everywhere, though she'd given up trying to tame it. We didn't say anything and it was…okay.

And weird. So weird because I couldn't get a read on this girl and I wanted to.

"I'm off shift at five," I told her. "Want to get together then? Before dinner?"

Annie shook her head. "I can't. That's usually when I… when we get ready."

Oh. Right. Guys took a ten-minute shower and they were good to go. Girls needed hours to shower, do their hair, do their makeup, pick out their clothes, and whatever else.

"I really don't want to have the lessons in the middle of the day, when everyone could, uh, see us together," she admitted, making a little face.

"Not like I could give you lessons in the middle of the day, since I'm usually out here." I waved a hand toward the lake. Figuring I'd better keep my head on the job and not on this girl who made me feel weird, I faced the lake fully, my gaze locked on the expanse of shimmering blue water, the multiple canoes and kayaks that were floating everywhere.

Plus, if my uncle caught me with Annie, he'd ask too many questions. Questions I didn't really want to answer.

"Oh." She hesitated. "True." She said nothing more and neither did I, so we sat there in silence for long, slightly uncomfortable minutes. I shoved my sunglasses back over my eyes so she couldn't get a read on them. On me. I didn't know why she remained up on the stand with me. I sort of wanted her gone. Yet another part of me wanted her to stay. Not because I was hoping to score with her, which was how I'd felt about Lacey at one point.

But this girl…I don't know. There was something about her that made me want to keep her around. I wanted to talk to her. Learn more about her. Maybe even give her grief in the hope that she'd dish some back out at me.

Weird, right? Totally weird. This girl was so far off my radar that she shouldn't even compute. She wasn't what I would call hot. She wasn't what I would call street-smart, either. She definitely wasn't looking for something casual with me. Annie would expect romance and flowers and moonlit walks and holding hands and cuddling on movie night and long, soft kisses that we both would never want to end…

I shook my head once, extra hard, to get the Disney fantasy out of my still-sleep-fogged brain. That was the only explanation for me thinking of actually kissing Annie.

"Don't you have an activity to go to? Like a Popsicle

house to make or something?" I finally asked, swiveling my head to glare at her. I was being an ass on purpose so hopefully I could get rid of her. She made me think strange thoughts. Made me want even stranger things.

I didn't like it.

Annie stood, wobbling a little on her feet, and for a brief, terrifying moment I had the image of her falling from the lifeguard tower and plummeting to the ground. I almost reached out to grab her.

"Why are you being such a jerk?" she asked, clearly confused. "I could tell your uncle about your little nap time out here. He'd probably be real mad at you."

Her confusion, the way she was looking at me, made me feel like shit. I shouldn't be so mean to her. Even if she just basically threatened me. "Sorry," I bit out, the word raspy. She had no idea what a big deal that just was. I never say sorry about anything. "Let's meet at eight o'clock at the pool, okay? How does that sound?"

Annie lifted her chin, her expression defiant. "Fine," she muttered. Without saying another word, she turned and climbed down the tower, her feet landing on the ground with a soft *thud* before she ran away.

. . .

## ANNIE

I waited by the pool, pacing the length of it back and forth, my flip-flops slapping against the ground. No one else was around, everyone was getting ready for movie night, and I wondered if it was a mistake, meeting Jake when I should be waiting for the signal from Kyle.

I ran into him on the way to the pool, and he'd given me the details. Everyone was meeting behind the arts and crafts building at nine fifteen. Lights-out was later on movie night, which gave us an extra hour to get drunk, according to Kyle, who'd grinned at me.

And I'd only grinned back like a fool, caught up in the light hazel color of his eyes. He was so freaking pretty...and then I remembered Jake's eyes. How dark they were. How they seemed to see right into me, like he understood me. I practically ran away from Kyle after that, barely caring if he wanted to talk to me or not.

All I could think about was Jake, which I realized, after leaving Kyle, was totally pointless.

Right?

He was late, which I guess shouldn't surprise me, but I was still disappointed. I needed these swim lessons. As silly as it sounded, the more confident I'd feel around water, the more confident I'd feel around Kyle. I knew this. Yeah, he was talking to me and wanting me to hang out with him while they all passed around a bottle of peppermint schnapps, but what if that was it? I needed to keep his interest, prove to him that I was strong and interesting and unafraid of anything.

I needed to convince myself of that, too.

Frowning, I glanced around, but I was still alone. I had no idea what time it was, since I didn't wear a watch and I didn't have my phone, but it felt like I'd been waiting for Jake for hours. That had to do more with my serious case of nerves versus how long I'd actually been waiting. I'd guess he was only about five minutes late.

He'd better show.

Kelsey was the one who'd coordinated my outfit. She pulled my hair into a topknot, made sure I remembered to wear earrings, and she put waterproof mascara on my eyelashes so if I actually got my face in the water—fat chance of that happening—then it wouldn't run. Then she chose what she deemed was my cutest bikini and had me wear a plain white T-shirt over it and a pair of black cotton shorts that I'd brought to wear to bed.

I worried the makeup might make it look like I was trying too hard, but as Kelsey put it, "If Jake becomes interested in you, then Kyle will be interested in you, and bam, you get exactly who you want." I didn't see Jake finding me appealing at all. I think I annoyed him more than anything. The feeling was mutual.

Mostly.

Who was I really trying to impress? Kyle or Jake? I wasn't even sure anymore.

Sighing loudly, I went to the gate and peeked over it, looking for him. Everyone was headed to movie night. Our cabin had already walked there and I'd walked with them, Kelsey whispering that she would cover for me if needed once I took off toward the pool. I didn't want anyone to notice I was gone, especially Hannah. I really liked her, despite her scary organizational skills and easy command of camp songs.

"Hey."

His deep voice startled me, and I turned on a gasp, my mouth dropping open when I saw him standing in front of me, his expression all business. He had on a white T-shirt that said "Camp Pine Ridge" that fit him to perfection. As in, it showcased his muscles without being too tight. And he'd changed out of the red lifeguard swim trunks, wearing a pair covered in a subtle blue-and-white Hawaiian print.

He looked…good, as much as I hated to admit it.

"Sorry I'm a little late," he said, offering no explanation. Not that it was any of my business, but I could tell he wasn't going to be friendly. He even looked a little irritated, and I guess I couldn't blame him. He'd probably rather do anything else but this.

"It's okay." I tried to smile, but it felt funny so I let it fade. "Are you ready?"

"Shouldn't I be asking you that?" When I said nothing,

he rolled his eyes. "Yeah, I'm ready. Let's do this." Without warning, he tore off his shirt and dropped it on a nearby chair. My gaze roamed over his bared chest, taking in every detail I could, which only left me feeling like a complete pervert. Thinking like that sent my blush into overdrive, and my cheeks felt like they were on fire.

Turning away from him, I went over to the lounge chairs and kicked my flip-flops underneath one. Then I pulled off my T-shirt, folding it carefully before I set it on the lounge chair. I quickly stepped out of my shorts and folded them as well. I swear I heard him laugh behind me, but I decided to ignore it. He could laugh all he wanted. I was the one who got her way, not him. I hoped he remembered that.

"Come on, let's go sit down," he said. I turned to watch him walk over to the shallow end of the pool. He sat on the edge and dunked his feet into the water. When I didn't so much as move from my spot, he waved a hand, indicating he wanted me to come sit by him. "Yo. Come here."

Reluctantly I went to join him, sitting close by but not right next to him, needing the distance. I didn't want him to get any weird ideas. "How is this part of my lesson?"

"So impatient." He shook his head, and I glared at him. "I'm not just going to push you into the water and expect you to learn how to swim, Annie. This is a gradual thing."

I lifted my chin. "My dad said when he was little, his father tossed him into a lake and basically said, 'Swim or die. It's your choice.'" That story had terrified me when I was a little kid, especially since I'd adored my grandpa so much.

"Cold," Jake said with a low whistle, his gaze meeting mine. "Tell me what you know about swimming."

I shrugged, feeling inadequate. "Not much. I don't really like the water."

"You're not even putting your feet in the pool," he pointed out.

He was right. I was sitting on the edge of the pool cross-legged. "It freaks me out."

"Let me guess. You don't like to get your hair wet."

I hated that he thought that way about me. I wasn't some vain girl obsessed with her appearance. I could get dirty when need be. But could I tell him the truth and know that he wouldn't reveal my secret? It was so…sad. It had happened so long ago, and I still wasn't over it.

"That's not it at all. Do I look like a girl who spends a lot of time on my hair?" I pointed at the messy knot on top of my head.

"Some girls spend hours trying to achieve that look."

"It took Kelsey two minutes to twist my hair like this."

"So if it's not that, then what is it?" He peered at me, ducking his head a little so that our gazes were even. "Are you scared of the water?"

I sank my teeth into my lower lip and gave a short nod.

"Did something happen to you? A bad experience when you were younger?"

I hadn't talked about what happened when I was a kid in a long time. No one really knew about it beyond my family, and it wasn't like we talked about it anymore. "When I was four. Yeah." I didn't need to share any more details. That would have to be enough. "But I don't want to talk about it."

"Fair enough." He looked down and swirled his feet in the water, churning it so little droplets hit my bent legs. "Why did you jump into the lake last night? If you're that scared and had a past bad experience?"

"I don't know…" My voice drifted. How could I explain I'd been seized with this need to prove to myself that I could do it? I'd wanted to impress Kyle and my new friends. I hadn't thought about the consequences or anything else and just… jumped. I'd always lived such a quiet, boring existence that for once in my life, I was actually dared to do something totally out of my comfort zone, and I'd wanted to shake it up.

He wouldn't understand. I had a feeling he knew nothing about boring existences or feeling the need to shake things up.

"It was a crazy move," he said. When I lifted my head to defend myself, I saw that he was smiling. "A ballsy move."

I shouldn't be glad he called me ballsy, but I was. No one had ever described me like that before, and up until that very moment, I wouldn't have considered it a compliment, either.

Now I did. "Ballsy" translated to "strong." And though my feminist side was stirring, a little irritated that balls equaled strength, I couldn't help but want to wear that word like a badge of honor.

So ridiculous.

"I'm hoping you can be ballsy again. I don't want to push you, but we won't be able to get much in with only a few lessons."

"I'm okay with that." At this point I had to take what I could get.

"Can I ask you another question before we get in the water?"

Oh, crap. We had to get in the water *tonight*? Why didn't I think this through? No way could I hop into the pool and act like it was no big deal. It was a *huge* deal, even if we were only going into the shallow end. At least we weren't in the lake, which was so cold and full of live creatures and the bottom was gross, sticky mud, but still.

"Go ahead. Ask me," I said, trying to sound cool. Like the idea of getting into the water with him didn't make my stomach twist and turn.

"Why are you pushing this on yourself so hard? Is there something you want to get over? A goal you have in mind? Do you want to go home and tell your parents you're a swimmer now? What's the deal?"

# Chapter Ten

### JAKE

I waited for her answer, still swirling my legs through the water, watching it spin and splash. I really wanted to kick water onto her just to ease the tension, but she'd probably freak. She'd looked scared out of her mind earlier when I asked if something had happened to her in the past. Whatever it was, it must've been awful. And she wasn't in the mood to share that old memory, either.

More like she didn't trust me with it. Fine. I didn't trust her, either, so we were even.

Kyle and his group of friends had smuggled in the booze, and he'd given me the details on the meeting place info, so I'd try to find them later once Annie and I were finished. I'd probably *need* to get my buzz on after dealing with teaching Annie how to swim.

If she could be that terrified of water yet pushed herself to jump into the lake in the middle of the night, she must've had a pretty damn good reason for wanting to learn to swim.

Why didn't she ever take lessons at home? Why did it have to be this summer at camp, when she suddenly felt the need to learn?

I didn't get it.

I wanted to get it.

"I don't want anyone else to make fun of me," she finally said, her voice barely above a whisper. I stopped kicking my feet in the water so I could hear her better. "Everyone can swim here."

"Not everyone," I started to say, but she quieted me with a look.

"Everyone above the age of *eight* can swim here. They're all so comfortable in the water, around the water. And I'm just…not. I don't want to stick out. I don't want people to ask uncomfortable questions that I don't know how to answer, or try to delve into my past to find out what the heck is wrong with me. I'm a—very private person." She clamped her lips shut and looked away from me.

"Well, come on. If I'm going to teach you some basics, we need to get on it. So far we've done nothing but sit around and waste time." I hopped into the pool, the water hitting me below the waist, like barely above my knees, and I waved at Annie to jump in and join me.

She sat frozen on the edge of the pool, her legs crossed like she was ready to bust out some yoga.

"Put your feet in the water," I told her, hoping she'd agree and just…do it. Helping Dewey out with some preliminary activities he liked to put the kids through if they needed lessons had taught me a thing or two. He'd have them kick the water. Then stand in the water. Then hold on to the edge of the pool and let their bodies stretch out before they started kicking. Then he'd bring out the kickboards and so on. It was a simple step-by-step process, gradually becoming harder and harder until they finally had to put their face in the water and actually, you know, swim.

I'd thought Dewey was a pain in the ass for making those kids go through all of those tedious steps. But now I saw there was a method to his madness. They needed to go through every one of those steps to slowly become more comfortable in the water. Had to give the guy props.

I also really wished he were right here, right now, taking this duty off my shoulders.

Slowly, without saying a word, not even looking at me, she untucked her feet from beneath her legs and let them dangle over the edge, though not close enough to actually touch the water. She inched her feet down slowly, scooting her butt closer to the ledge so she would have no choice but to finally dunk those feet and get them wet.

Yet she still didn't make a move, her feet hovering over the water. Frustration rippled through me. I was trying to be on my best behavior, but it was kind of hard. I wasn't the most patient person in the world.

Annie dipped a toe—no joke, just her big toe—in the water, pulling her foot back so fast, it was like it never happened. She tucked the water-tainted foot beneath her bent leg, contemplating the situation in front of her, nibbling on her lower lip. Something she did whenever she was nervous, I'd noticed. She looked ready to bolt, and I needed to convince her to stay. "I don't want to do this," she admitted, her voice small.

"You have to." *Why the hell am I trying to convince her?*

She shook her head. Didn't say anything.

"It can't be that bad. The water's not even that deep." I paused, but she still said nothing. "Annie. Look at me." I waded into the deeper end, feeling the water rise, enjoying the sensation as it swirled around me. When I finally made it to the point where my feet were no longer touching the bottom and I was treading water, I turned to look at Annie.

"If I can do this, you can definitely dunk your feet," I said, making it sound like a challenge.

Her brows rose. This girl loved a challenge. She started all over again, the second time around just as painful as the first, as she carefully inched her foot forward, excruciatingly slow just like the last time. Until finally, those toes were in the water—then her entire foot was in the water and she was squealing and I started shouting my encouragement, telling her she's got this. All she needed was a little push.

I wanted to be the one who pushed her. She didn't seem to mind, either. Despite the squealing and the yelling, she was giggling, her eyes sparkling, and she looked so pretty I got sort of lost in the moment.

Until I realized we were causing such a major scene surely someone could hear us.

I immediately went quiet and so did she, each of us staring at the other until she burst out laughing, her hand going to her mouth to stifle the sound. She slipped her other foot into the water without any urging, and I grinned in return, flicking my chin at her. "Get all the way in the water, Annie."

Her legs went still, her hands braced on the edge of the pool. Without thought I let my gaze wander the length of her. She was slightly bent over, her position offering me the perfect glimpse of her chest. She had a nice one. She had a nice everything, and the realization shocked me.

My dad told me when I was around thirteen that I should watch out for the quiet girls. "They'll sneak up on you and blow your mind. Not only are they smart and won't put up with any of your shit, but they're usually beautiful, too. You just don't realize how perfect they are because they're so damn quiet all the time. They'll sneak their way right into your heart. Once that happens, you're done for," he'd said.

At the time, I thought he was full of crap. What did he know about the quiet ones? They were boring.

But now, staring at Annie, thinking about how she was sneaking up on me and she didn't even know it, I realized that maybe he was right.

Which meant I was totally done for.

• • •

## ANNIE

I didn't like the way Jake was watching me. It was like I could feel his gaze on every part of me, like he was giving me a full examination with his eyes, and it made me uncomfortable. I'd never been so blatantly checked out before in my life.

Every time I got around Kyle, I was nervous. But Jake? He made me feel more than nervous. He made me feel all jumpy and weird and…excited.

I didn't like it.

My feet were still in the water, and it wasn't so bad. I'd rather jump in the way I had at the lake than continue to have Jake stare at me, so I did just that. Pushed myself off the edge of the pool and hopped in, the water coming to about my waist. I sucked in a sharp breath, shocked by the water's cool temperature. Shocked even more that I was standing in the water voluntarily.

"Good job," Jake said. "Now walk toward me."

"I'm not going into the deep end," I told him, shaking my head.

"I get it. Just…walk as far as you feel comfortable with. You can stop whenever you want."

He was still treading water but he moved closer, until his feet must've hit the bottom, though the water was still up to his neck. He remained there, watching me, murmuring little words of encouragement as I hesitantly started to move forward. Taking it one step at a time, the water almost feeling like it wanted to drag me down, but I resisted.

I needed to do this.

So I pushed forward, taking a few more steps until the water reached just beneath my armpits. My breathing was shaky and my heart raced and this was as far as I could go before I'd lose it. "I'm going to stop," I told him, and he drifted closer, so he stood directly in front of me.

Jake was much taller than I was, so when his feet touched the bottom, the water only hit him at rib level. Meaning I was getting an up-close-and-personal view of his lean chest. I could see the definition of the muscles in his arms, and he wasn't even doing anything. He had a nice body, not too muscly or overblown. I bet he gave good hugs.

I blinked, pushing the thought out of my head.

"You went pretty far," he said, his lips curved in a closed-mouth smile. "I'm impressed."

The compliment filled me with pride. I really needed to hear that. "Thanks."

"Can you put your head underwater?"

"No." Just the thought filled me with icy-cold panic.

"Would you feel comfortable holding on to the edge of the pool and kicking in the water?"

I shrugged, struggling with embarrassment. He must have thought I was the most immature failure in the whole wide world. "I can try."

He nodded. "Good. Let's go."

Jake was actually a really good teacher. I appreciated his patience, and he thankfully didn't make me feel stupid. His gentle encouragement calmed my fears, and he stood next to me the entire time while I clung to the edge of the pool and kicked my legs in the water, listening to him count my kicks and telling me I shouldn't give up.

It almost felt like he was my coach or something, which I knew was kind of stupid, but whatever worked, right?

"Okay, I think we're done for the night," he said after my

fourth round of kicks. "I think you did pretty well."

He stood next to me, my fingers still curled around the concrete edge and my body buoyant in the water. "You really think so?"

"Yeah. I do." He nodded, then turned toward the small building that stood next to the pool. "We've already been out here for almost an hour."

"How do you know?"

"There's a clock right over there." He pointed at the giant clock that hung on the side of the building, under the overhang where towels were stored and disbursed.

Oh. The clock I never even noticed. The clock he'd probably been staring at the entire time, dying to get this lesson over with so he could go hang out with his friends or whatever.

"Okay. Well, thanks." I settled my feet on the bottom of the pool and waited for him to get out first. No way was I going to climb out of this pool just for him to catch me at a weird angle.

"One lesson down." He waved a hand toward the short ladder that led out of the pool. "Ladies first."

I sent him an incredulous look. Yeah right, he's a gentleman. "It's okay. You go ahead."

He rolled his eyes. "Go, Annie."

Ugh. He wasn't letting me off the hook. I went over to the narrow little stepladder thing that led out of the pool and grabbed hold of the silver handles, hoisting myself up and out of the water. I silently hoped he wasn't checking out my butt—what if I had a wedgie and half my bottoms were lodged between my cheeks?

I scurried over to the shelf where the towels were kept and grabbed one, wrapping it tightly around my dripping body. I needed to get back over to movie night. I hadn't seen Kelsey, so I figured Hannah hadn't noticed I was missing. Yet.

"I should go," I said as I turned around to catch Jake standing right next to me, rubbing his chest with a towel.

I averted my gaze. Wow, this just felt way too personal. Or maybe I was just overreacting.

"Yeah. Go. Wanna meet tomorrow night? Same time, same place?"

"Do you?" I asked incredulously, turning to face him once more.

"Yeah." He nodded. "The quicker we get this over with, the better, right?"

Ouch. Right. I needed to remember that he was doing this reluctantly. Not like he wanted to really help me or anything. "Right," I said firmly, heading over to the lounger to grab my clothes. "Guess I'll see you tomorrow."

"Tomorrow," he echoed after me.

# Chapter Eleven

Jake

"You made it! Glad you're here, bro." Kyle clapped me on the back, shooting a grin to all of his friends—most of them guys from his cabin—before he turned that giant smile on me, the bottle of schnapps clutched in his hand. He waved it at me. "Want some?"

I glanced around, hating how close my uncle's office was. "I thought the plan was to sneak off first and then drink." Drinking in the woods was much safer than drinking behind the arts and crafts building, for the love of God. Not that these idiots would realize that. From the way it appeared, they'd been passing the bottle around a while. "We'd be better off by the lake."

We had no idea where Uncle Bob was. He could pop out of his office door at any time, though he was probably back at his cabin and already asleep.

Still. I didn't want to take any chances. Not when everything was at stake. My uncle catches me and I'm headed straight to juvenile hall. No house arrest for me; the judge had made that clear. I needed to stay clean and not do anything stupid.

But I must be an idiot like the rest of these guys because here I was, not moving, ready to get my drink on.

"Nah, forget that plan. It'll take too long to get to the woods, and there are a few people at the lake already. Bunch of snitches, too." Kyle laughed, and so did the other guys. "Some of the girls from G7A and B are out there. We don't need the aggravation."

More like they didn't want to share the schnapps. I wondered if Annie was out there. Or maybe she was going to hang out with us, though I doubted this was really her scene. "We get caught, we're done for," I reminded them, glancing over my shoulder at the main office. The light still shone where my uncle's secretary worked, but I didn't think she was still there. Though maybe she was. Hell, maybe he was, too. I couldn't be sure.

"Stop being such a downer. We're ready to get our party on right now." Kyle brought the bottle to his lips and took a swig before Blake—the one who brought the booze in the first place—swiped the bottle from him. "Saw you chatting up the new girl earlier."

Unease filled me. "Who are you talking about?"

"You know who. The new girl. Whatever her name is." Kyle flicked his hair out of his eyes, a habit I found freaking annoying. "I can't remember. I'm blaming the schnapps." He cracked up, like what he said was so damn funny.

It wasn't. I was irritated. He couldn't even remember her name? She was totally hot for him, and he barely knew she existed. "Her name is Annie," I said through my clenched teeth.

"Right. Annie." Kyle snapped his fingers. "Annie, Amy, something like that."

Jackass.

"Saw you two talking by the lake. Like, she was up in the tower with you." Kyle tilted his head to the side, immediately reminding me of a dog. My dog looked at me like that when he was confused by whatever I was saying. And I'm pretty sure my dog was smarter than Kyle. "You two got something going on or what?"

"Who, me and Annie?" I laughed, but not too forcefully. I didn't want to look like I was faking it—even though I was. "We're just friends."

"Gotcha." Kyle flicked his hair out of his eyes again. "Good to know."

No one said anything as we continued to pass the bottle around. I couldn't speak, my mind twisted over the many things Kyle could want from Annie. The girl whose name he didn't even know. He must like her. She liked him, so her wish would come true. She'd probably end up with Kyle this summer; they could have a cute little camp romance and then go their separate ways come August.

Just the thought left a sour feeling in my stomach.

"I invited Annie to join us tonight, though I'm starting to think she's gonna chicken out."

My entire body went stiff at the mention of her name. "So what's going on with you two? You like her?" I asked, trying my best to keep my voice even. I shouldn't be jealous. I had no reason to be jealous. I wasn't interested in her, not like that.

"I guess." Kyle shrugged. "Everyone else here is been there, done that, you know what I mean? I always approve of new blood."

"What about the redhead, her friend?" Blake asked, passing the bottle to someone else. "She's pretty new, too."

"I don't like redheads. They're not my type." Kyle's mouth stretched into that stupid grin again. I could tell he was already feeling the alcohol, the lightweight. "I do like blondes, though.

I like blondes a lot."

I took the bottle that was passed to me and looked around before I took a quick drink. I freaking needed it after hearing Kyle talk about Annie and how he liked blondes. What the hell ever. I only planned on having a few drinks and then I was out of here. Couldn't chance sticking around for too long. What if Uncle Bob came across us? I'd get sent home, no questions asked. My dad would be so pissed he wouldn't bother sending me to juvie. He'd murder me in my sleep and it would be rest in peace, Jake.

After my court appearance, he'd reminded me how much a record could possibly ruin my chances at getting into the university of my choice. College was my ticket out of there. One more year of high school and then I was free—unless I screwed everything up.

Forget that shit. Couldn't risk it.

"Can I be honest?" I asked Kyle.

He nodded. "Go for it."

"I don't think she's your type," I told him after I took a second swig and passed him the bottle.

Kyle frowned. "Why do you say that?"

"Because. She's too…" *Sweet. Cute. Nice. Innocent.* I couldn't say any of that.

"Virginal?" Blake supplied for me, making all of them start laughing.

"Totally," another one of them shouted, nudging Kyle in the ribs. He just pushed the guy off with a shake of his head.

"I could get into that," he said with a slight sneer, his eyes glassy. "All the ladies love me."

"Egotistical asshole," I muttered under my breath, which only made Kyle laugh louder. At least the guy knew what he was and had no shame.

"Seriously. She's not your type." I clapped him on the shoulder and gave him a quick shake. "You'll try to kiss her and she'll probably jump a mile."

"Nah, that's just if you tried, Fazio, what with that serial killer stare you got going on," Kyle said. "You need to lighten up, bro. Seriously."

Serial killer stare? This guy was seriously a jerk. "Whatever, man. Just think twice before you attempt to make a move on Annie. She's probably not up to your speed."

I turned on my heel to go, muttering a good-bye to no one, considering not a one of them was listening, and as I rounded the arts and crafts building, I ran smack into a small, soft body.

A small, soft body who reached out and shoved me away from her. Hard.

"Hey, watch it—" I started to yell, my lips clamping shut when I saw who it was.

Annie.

"You all right?" I changed my tone, softening my voice. I didn't want to scare her. "Sorry about that. I didn't see you."

She said nothing. Just wrapped her arms around herself, the hurt look in her eyes telling me all I needed to know without her saying a single word.

I'd bet big money she'd overheard our conversation and all the shitty things I said. All the shitty things Kyle said, too.

Great.

She dodged out of my reach when I tried to grab her arm, her pained gaze turning hostile in a quick second. "Don't touch me," she whisper-hissed.

I was at a complete loss as to what I should do. I'd blown it. She'd heard me say he should stay away from her. Had heard us bag on the fact that she was too virginal. That was mean. I couldn't take any of it back. But at least I could offer her up a bit of advice.

So I did.

"Don't go meet him," I told her as she turned away from me. "Ditch him tonight, Annie."

She paused, glancing over her shoulder at me. "Why should I listen to you? From what I heard, he wants me there."

"Right. And if you don't show up, he'll want you even more." I was surprised I could force the words out of my throat. "We always want what we can't have, right?"

Yeah. Wasn't that the truth? Because right now, as I stood there in front of Annie and looked at her pretty face, I couldn't help but think...

*I want her.*

*Yet I can't have her.*

"You're making a valid point." She lifted her nose into the air, all haughty princess.

"I can give you more pointers," I told her.

She lifted her brows. "What do you mean?"

"Tomorrow. At your next swim lesson. You want to get with Kyle?" Just saying the words made my stomach churn. Totally over-the-top reaction but hey, I was being honest with myself. If I couldn't have her, then I could help her with Kyle, and once they ended up together, then I'd leave her alone.

And I needed to leave her alone. She was too...tempting.

Annie nodded, nibbling on her lower lip.

"Then take my advice. Don't go meet him right now. Not like you'll get to talk to him much anyway. He's back there with all of his friends." My heart was galloping like I just ran a marathon. I didn't want her hanging out with Kyle. Not tonight. He was already buzzed. What if he made a move on her? I'd never forgive myself if something bad happened to her...

Not that I thought Kyle was a bad guy, but he was drunk. Who knew what he might do?

"Fine." She sighed and threw her hands up in the air. "I won't go."

Relief filled my chest, easing my erratically thumping heart. Thank God she listened to me.

"But you owe me tips. Pointers." She pointed right at me. "You're going to help me convince Kyle that we'd be a good match. And you're not going to tell anyone about this, either. None of this."

She sure was a bossy little thing. I kind of liked it. Standing straight, I saluted her. "Yes, ma'am."

A little smile curled her lips, but she hid it, her expression turning serious. "Same time tomorrow?"

"Same time tomorrow," I agreed.

"See you at the pool." She walked away before I could say anything else.

· · ·

## ANNIE

I was probably a complete idiot to agree with Jake to not go meet Kyle last night. I'd been nervous about it, afraid of who would be there, scared I'd say something stupid and ruin everything. I hadn't wanted to drink. If I was going to do it, I didn't want my first real drinking experience to be with me and a bunch of guys I didn't really know. That was like every teen movie come to life.

This was the summer of being brave, not being stupid.

Plus, as mad at Jake as I was last night, his words had actually made sense. We always want what we can't have. If I were always eager and saying yes to Kyle's every request, he'd tire of me fast. If I played hard to get, he'd work that much harder to, ahem, get me.

So yeah. I was totally on board with Jake's plan. More on board with him giving me pointers and helping me gain Kyle's attention. I wasn't exactly sure why he offered, but he'd seemed almost…concerned about me last night. Like he really hadn't wanted me to go hang out with Kyle at all. Was he watching out for me? Worried about my safety?

That was sort of...touching. Even though I was still irritated over what he said to Kyle and all the other boys. And Kyle had been rude, too. I didn't know what to think. Was it the alcohol talking? Or were they all just jerks?

It was game night tonight, and I didn't care if I was a little late to that. They'd held game night the second night I was at camp, and it was nothing but chaos the entire time. No one would miss me, and besides, Kelsey was covering for me again.

As I pushed through the gate and approached the pool, I realized that I didn't feel as apprehensive when I saw the water. Last night I could barely look at the pool, I was so nervous.

Maybe I was already making progress.

"You're late."

I whirled around to find Jake kicked back on one of the loungers, shirtless and wearing those same blue Hawaiian-print swim trunks from last night, his arms bent behind his head, his biceps bulging. My heart flipped over itself seeing him like that, all relaxed and cute and oh my God, I really needed to stop thinking about Jake that way.

Counselors didn't go out with campers. Plus, Jake was too intense, too much for me. I didn't care how sweet or helpful he'd been. Kyle was more my speed, more my taste.

Glancing at the clock, I rolled my eyes at him. "It's only one minute after eight."

"Still counts as late." He leaped to his feet and sauntered over to where I stood, reaching out to tug on the ends of my ponytail. "You ready to do this?"

Mute, I nodded. He was terribly close. I could smell him, all soapy clean and fresh. He had a baseball cap on backward and he grabbed the bill at the back of his head, flipped the hat off, and tossed it onto a nearby chair. I watched the hat fall, almost afraid to look anywhere else, because I had the distinct feeling he was totally checking me out.

And I was totally letting him.

"Take your dress off, then, and let's go." He strode toward the pool, and I watched him go, my gaze locked on his back. I'd never given a guy's back much thought before. Jake's was smooth-skinned and tan from the sun, his muscles shifting with his every movement. His shoulders were impossibly broad and his hips were narrow and those swim trunks hung a little low. Almost scandalously low.

My entire body went hot from the direction my thoughts just went, and I shook my head once, telling myself to get over it, get over Jake. This was about snagging Kyle. Getting him interested in me. I didn't need to have distracting thoughts about a counselor. Relationships between counselors and campers were strictly off-limits, and I wasn't about to get in trouble.

I shrugged out of my swimsuit cover-up and made my way toward the pool, sitting on the edge of the shallow end and immediately dunking my feet into the water. Jake sat down right next to me. So close our shoulders bumped.

"Impressive," he murmured, his gaze meeting mine.

I looked away from those dark, all-seeing eyes, studying the water instead. "I don't have much time, so I need to push myself to get over my fears."

"You don't want to push yourself too hard, though. That could only set you back," he pointed out.

I slid my gaze to his once more, defiant. "I won't set myself back. I can't afford to."

"Fair enough." He nodded, then rubbed his hands together. The movement caused our shoulders to bump into each other again, and I noticed how warm his skin was. "Let's jump in."

He splashed into the water and turned to face me, his disappointment clear. I knew he fully expected me to follow after him, and I'd wanted to. Believe me, I would've done it, but the thought of actually hopping into the water without someone or something to catch me just sort of seized me up.

So I remained frozen by the edge of the pool instead.

"Come on, Annie," he said, his voice low. Coaxing. "Join me."

I shook my head, not able to put into words my stupid, paralyzing fears. It was so frustrating, how one second I felt perfectly fine and the next I wanted to bolt.

He held his arms out, like I was a toddler ready to jump toward him. "You can do it." He waggled his fingers at me.

"No." I shook my head again, the ends of my ponytail whapping my cheeks, making me wince. Who knew hair could feel so sharp?

"Annie." His voice became stern. "You can do this. I know you can. Just…jump."

"I can't," I whispered, my body starting to shake.

"You can," he countered, his voice, his gaze, gentle. "I'll catch you. I promise."

Why did the thought of feeling his strong, muscled arms wrapped around me and holding me tight make my skin tingle?

"If you jump in, I'll tell you everything I know about your boyfriend, Kyle," he all but singsonged.

*He's not my boyfriend,* I wanted to say, but I didn't bother correcting him. I started to laugh, irritated at myself that his offer was actually working. "Really?"

He nodded, trying his best to hold back a smile. He had a nice smile, big and warm and friendly.

Gripping the edge of the pool, I leaned forward and took a deep breath, my gaze lifting to Jake's. His eyes were locked on my chest and I glanced down, saw the way my position gave me some major cleavage. Warmth bloomed deep within me that he was actually checking me out. Little ol' me, Annie the nobody.

With Jake, I never felt like a nobody.

I let go of the rounded edge and practically belly flopped into the pool, sucking in a sharp breath when I made contact with the water. Gasped even more when I felt those strong arms envelop me and pull me into his hot, hard chest.

"You did it," he murmured close to my ear. "Look at you, jumping into the water like it's no big deal."

I blinked up at him, water clinging to my eyelashes, sliding down my cheeks. I hadn't gone underwater, but I'd caused a big enough splash to douse Jake and myself. We were incredibly close, like intimate-hug and he-could-kiss-me close, and I stared up at him, cataloging his every feature. His thick, dark eyebrows and his warm brown eyes surrounded by the thickest eyelashes I'd ever seen. His nose was just the slightest bit crooked, hooking to the right, and he had a tiny scar on his left cheek, another one just below the center of his bottom lip.

How did he get those scars? I wanted to know.

His breath fanned across my face, minty fresh like he must've just brushed his teeth or was chewing gum, and I closed my eyes for the briefest moment, trying to calm the swirl of confusion running through my brain.

"He likes to tell dirty jokes."

I opened my eyes, frowning at Jake in confusion. "Who does?"

He sent me a look, one that said *duh*. "Kyle. The dirtier the better."

My nose wrinkled. "Ew."

He chuckled. "I know."

"What else?" I asked as he righted me, his hands going to my waist as I let my legs drop, my feet touching the ground. We were still in the shallow end, and the water came to my waist. The sky was dimming quickly, the sun long gone, and it was dark outside. Quiet. It was like we were the only two out here.

"His parents are filthy rich."

I already figured out that much. Everything Kyle owned seemed to have a designer logo on it. "And…"

"His middle name is Richard."

Well. That was kind of cute.

"Otherwise known as Dick," he said with a straight face.

"Now who's the crude one?" I asked, giving Jake a shove, though he didn't move a muscle. He just grinned at me in response. "What's your middle name?"

His grin faded. "Robert."

"Jacob Robert Fazio," I murmured thoughtfully, realization dawning. "Wait, as in…"

"Uncle Bob. Robert Fazio. Fozzie Bear. My dad wanted to name me after his big brother," Jake explained.

Aw, that was sweet. Even sweeter? Jake seemed kind of embarrassed. His cheeks were ruddy, and now he wouldn't look at me. Though he was still holding on to me, his hands on my waist, my hands on his arms. He was touching nothing but bare skin, a place no one else had ever really touched before, and for some weird reason it didn't feel unnatural or wrong.

It felt almost…right.

"Annie. I want you to hold on to my arms and float on your stomach," he instructed, his voice firm. He was back in teacher mode. "And kick your legs."

I stared up at him like I couldn't understand what he just said.

"Go on," he encouraged. "Float. I've got you."

We went on like that for at least ten minutes, Jake encouraging me to kick my legs as he dragged me all over the shallow end of the pool. I gripped his forearms tight for fear he might accidentally let me go, but he never did. Didn't complain, either, when surely I was hurting him, my nails digging little crescent moons into his skin.

"Loosen your hold on me," he eventually said, and reluctantly, I did. My hands slid down his arms, until his hands were curling around mine and I was still somehow miraculously floating. "Look at you. I bet I could let go and you'd swim on your own."

I immediately landed on my feet and let go of his hands, not missing the disappointment on his face. I ignored it and instead wanted to push him for more Kyle information.

That's why I was there, right? Not only for lessons but to learn everything he knew about Kyle.

"Does he have a girlfriend?" I asked.

Jake frowned, looking confused. "Who? Me? No, I don't."

My heart flipped. Yeah, I liked knowing that way too much. "Not you. Kyle."

"Oh." His expression switched. Now he was irritated. "No. He never has girlfriends."

"Wait a minute. How do you know?" It's not like Jake and Kyle were good friends. Yeah, they seemed friendly, but Jake had been at camp only a month longer than I had. How would he know much about Kyle?

"He told me so." Jake looked away, a warm wind suddenly washing over us, making his hair flutter over his forehead. "I think our lesson is done for the night. Don't you?"

"Um, okay. Sure." I ignored the disappointment that filled me and made a mad dash for the ladder, climbing out of the pool as quickly as I could and grabbing a towel so I could wrap it around me. Jake remained in the water, drifting closer to the deep end, and I watched him, frowning when he still didn't get out of the pool. "Aren't you coming out?"

"I don't think so. You go on, Annie. I'll see you around." He ducked under the water and began to swim in earnest. His arms sliced through the water, his legs kicking up a huge splash, and I watched him for a while, impressed with his speed, his pure determination seeming to propel him across the length of the pool and back.

He didn't talk to me. So after waiting around for a few minutes, I reluctantly left the pool area and went in search of my friends. Trying to ignore the confusion over my feelings toward Jake that lingered.

But it was hard. He remained on my mind the rest of the night, even when I tried to go to sleep.

I was starting to think it wasn't Kyle I liked at all.

# Chapter Twelve

I went in search of Annie, frustration filling me when I couldn't find her anywhere. I needed to start my lifeguard tower shift in less than fifteen minutes and I had no freaking clue where she was.

Luckily enough, I ran into some of the girls who were in her cabin out by the volleyball court.

"Hey!" I shouted at them, crooking my finger when they all turned to look at me, their brows lowered in puzzlement. "Come here."

They bounded over to where I stood, all four of them like they were a pack or a herd or something. I had no idea what their names were, not that it really mattered. "What's going on?" one of them asked.

I could see the curiosity blazing in their eyes. I was opening myself up to all sorts of questions—and rumors—by talking to them. But I had no choice. "I'm hoping maybe one of you, uh, knows where Annie is?"

They all turned to each other, matching smirks on their faces before another one of them said, "She's in the arts and crafts building."

Relief flooding me, I took off, yelling a thanks over my shoulder as I did so. I could hear them laughing behind me, but I didn't care. I needed to talk to Annie, and it couldn't wait much longer.

I'd sort of avoided her the past two days, which wasn't cool. But that last night together in the pool, the more we talked, the madder I got. Worse, I'd felt *jealous* over her constant questions about Kyle. I knew she liked him. Hell, I lured her into the pool with promises of information on Kyle. And then when I had to give up the goods, see that dreamy look glaze her eyes every time she said his name, I don't know. It made me…angry.

Jealous, too. And I never felt jealous. It was hard for me to admit even to myself that I was jealous of Kyle. The guy was a selfish idiot. He didn't care about anyone else, especially Annie. He didn't even remember her *name*.

That tool wasn't worth the ground she freaking walked on.

Not that I could tell her, or do anything about it. Not that I could say to her that I liked her. I couldn't like her. She was off-limits.

Forbidden.

At one point late last night when I couldn't sleep, I wondered if that made her even more attractive, the forbidden part. And how totally messed up that was. Could it be true? Was I proving the point that we want what we can't have?

I wasn't sure.

Despite my wariness, and my avoiding her, I missed her. A lot. I wanted to continue giving her those stupid swimming lessons. I wanted to make her smile and encourage her to keep going and see the flush of pleasure sweep across her cheeks when I told her she did a good job. Seeing her so happy did something to my chest that made it feel tight, like I could hardly breathe.

Truth? My reaction to her made me uncomfortable. I wasn't used to feeling like this, like I wanted something—someone—I couldn't have. I'd been angry and sad before, when I lost my mom and wanted her back so damn bad. I was pissed at everyone and for a while there, it felt like my world was coming to an end. But eventually I moved on because I had to. Life didn't let you stop no matter how hard you tried to make it slow down. I realized that quickly.

The death of my mother was the only thing I could relate to my confusing feelings for Annie, which messed with my head even more. How could losing my mom compare to losing any and all potential contact with Annie? I knew I wasn't in love with her—how could I be? I barely knew her. But maybe she was the first girl who'd entered my life that could possibly matter.

And I didn't know what to do with that.

"Relationships can cause problems, especially if you're in a position of authority," Uncle Bob had advised me when I first arrived. "If you want to…date a counselor, I have no problem with that as long as it doesn't affect your ability to work. Though honestly, I'd discourage you from getting yourself involved in any sort of relationship with a counselor. You need to keep your head on straight this summer and not get into trouble. That's why I need to tell you up front—if you're interested in a camper, it can't happen, Jake. They're taboo. And don't you forget it."

His words had stuck with me all through the first session. There weren't any campers who caught my interest, because I wouldn't let it happen. And then I met Annie and though at first I'd found her a pain in the ass more than anything, she grew on me. To the point that I couldn't stop thinking about her…

I'd thrown myself into work, trying to focus on what I needed to do versus what I wanted to do. I started assisting Dewey again with the beginners' swim lessons twice a week in the mornings. I helped Brian with the bonfire pit for the night activities. Just last night I told a ghost story, scaring the crap out of the ten-year-olds so that they ran shrieking for their cabin.

That had been fun. Brian and I got a good laugh out of that one. Even Uncle Bob had chuckled, telling me later that he was glad that I was "coming around."

Whatever that meant.

When the arts and crafts building came into view, I slowed down, going over in my mind exactly how I should approach her. I didn't really want to barge into the room and go right up to her. I didn't want to cause a scene. Subtlety was the name of the game.

I slipped just inside the building, remaining against the back wall where no one really noticed me. Nancy was at her desk, her head bent as she assembled something. My gaze searched the room, trying to find Annie's familiar blond head, and when I finally found her, the ache in my heart that I didn't know was there suddenly eased.

She was sitting at the table near the front of the room, putting together what looked like a picture frame made out of Popsicle sticks. Well, she was really helping out, since every table had an older camper sitting at it, assisting the younger kids with their Popsicle stick projects. Forgetting my subtlety plan, I went straight to her table and stood behind her, waiting for her to look up and acknowledge me. But she wouldn't, though I knew she saw me. I could tell by the subtle shift of her head in my direction.

She kept her gaze locked on the half-completed picture frame in front of her, her voice pitched unnaturally high as she talked to one of the girls she was helping. Her hands started to shake when she tried to straighten out a crooked Popsicle stick in her frame, and I gave in, both hating and liking that I made her so nervous.

"I need to tell you something, Annie," I said.

Her head still bent, she murmured, "Go away."

Hurt, I blew out a harsh breath and knelt beside her, not caring who was watching. I saw another set of girls from her cabin sitting at the other tables, their eyes wide as they studied us together. I was giving them a full show for their gossipy conversations over dinner later, but I didn't really care. I needed to talk to Annie before I started my shift. "I know we haven't talked the last few days but I've been busy."

She turned her head toward me, her gaze meeting mine for what felt like the first time in forever. Looking into those pretty, dark blue eyes made my chest ache. "Busy doing what? Avoiding me?"

I chuckled, surprised and impressed at her calling me out. "Maybe."

I started to stand, but she grabbed my hand, pulling me back down beside her. "I need to help everyone finish their projects first before I can talk to you."

"Right, because Popsicle stick picture frames are coveted works of art." I snorted. She glared, and I immediately regretted my crappy remark. "Sorry. I need to get to work, so I don't have much time."

Her expression softened, though I could still see the anger in her gaze. "What did you want to talk to me about, anyway?"

I glanced around, then lowered my voice. "I can't really say in front of everyone else."

She sent me a withering glance before she looked away. Like she didn't believe me.

Scooting closer, I pushed myself in between her chair and the girl sitting next to her, offering an *excuse me* when I bumped into the other girl. I leaned my arm across the table, my hand close to Annie's as I leaned in and whispered near her ear, "I'm sorry."

Her head jerked toward mine, her face close. Kissing close. Not that I was about to do anything like that in the middle of arts and crafts. "That's not going to get you off the hook." Her voice trembled.

I moved in even closer, tilting my head so I could breathe in the scent of her hair. I knew I'd missed her, but having her so near was making me think all sorts of thoughts. Bad ones. Ones I couldn't act on because fraternizing with campers was taboo. "We agreed earlier that I'd give you a swim lesson tonight, but I can't make it," I murmured as I reluctantly pulled away from her.

"Whatever." She looked away, her expression irritated, and my stomach churned.

She seemed mad. And it felt like I could do nothing right.

"I have to help lead the hike tonight." I really didn't want to do it, but my uncle pretty much said I had to. It was an annual thing, and they needed every counselor on duty. Even Dane had to work it.

She still said nothing.

I stood, my neck bent so I could keep watching her. "Come on, Annie. Talk to me."

Glancing up, she stared at me quietly. It was like the entire room had become quiet. Even Nancy was watching us with unmistakable interest.

My coming in here was probably not the smartest move.

I walked away from her table without a word and went to the other side of the room. A countertop ran the entire stretch of the far wall, shelves and cubbies below filled with all sorts of crafting stuff. A row of narrow shelves housed colorful construction paper, and I pulled a bright blue piece out of its slot.

A jar of markers stood nearby, and I grabbed a black pen, uncapped it, and wrote a quick note, pausing as I pondered each word I wanted to say. For once, I cared. I didn't want to screw this up.

Putting the pen away, I folded the paper into an airplane, taking my time as I carefully pressed each fold into the paper so the thing would fly properly.

If it didn't, I'd feel like a jackass.

Once I'd deemed it good enough, I strode back across the room, closer to Annie's table, and held the paper airplane between my fingers, practicing my throw. Working up the courage. I glanced around, saw that a few other girls from Annie's cabin were blatantly watching me, and I knew this story would definitely be around the camp by the end of the night. Uncle Bob would probably know all about it, too.

But screw it. I might look bad, doing this. I should walk away and forget about the brief time I spent with Annie, but I couldn't. I couldn't think about breaking the rules, about forbidden relationships. The minute I saw her, saw how hurt and angry she was, I had to get back into her good graces. I wanted to spend more time with her. Tomorrow, I would. Tonight, I had to help lead the hike. Tomorrow night would be about Annie. Helping her. Making her smile.

I aimed the airplane toward her pretty blond head and let it sail through the air. It landed on top of the table, right beside her elbow, and she glanced down at it before she turned in her chair and looked back at me, surprise lighting her eyes.

Flicking my chin at her, I turned and left the room.

Now it was on her.

· · ·

## ANNIE

I stared at the carefully folded paper airplane, tilted on its side where it rested on the table, right on top of my lame Popsicle stick picture frame.

It was from Jake.

I couldn't believe he'd come into the building like he did, like some sort of determined hero straight out of a romance novel, demanding that I talk to him. I'd been so embarrassed, I couldn't even look at him, and once I finally did, he flat out took my breath away, which was so confusing, I didn't know how to react or what to say.

He was wearing a white T-shirt with bold red lettering across the chest that said "lifeguard," and he had on the red shorts. He was somehow tanner than the last time I'd seen him, and he'd had his sunglasses shoved on top of his head, something he seemed to do a lot.

That I knew this tiny detail about him was…weird. Right? I shouldn't pay attention to those tiny details. I didn't like Jake. Not like that.

I was supposed to like Kyle. I mean, everyone was trying to put us together—even Jake!—and I appreciated their matchmaking efforts. I'd spent an hour with Kyle yesterday. We hung out during free time, and he was trying to make me laugh with his—yep, Jake had been right—really bad, super-dirty jokes, but I hadn't found them funny. He even tried to get me to help him play some pranks on the counselors, and at first I was game. Until he wanted me to sneak into Dane's cabin and steal his underwear. I don't mind playing harmless pranks, but stealing a grown man's underwear?

Um, no thanks.

Gwen had finally rescued me, muttering something about guys who were totally beneath me, and how I was wasting my time. She was probably right, but I'd been determined to focus on Kyle, especially since Jake was ignoring me.

I'd even hung out at the pool, staying in the shallow end and practicing my kicking. I'd been with the younger kids so no one really said anything. I'd pretended I was helping the kids out, and we kicked up such a huge splash I had all of them laughing and demanding more.

So I'd stayed with them for more than an hour. Even doggy-paddled around the shallow end. I couldn't believe it.

Jake would've been so proud of me.

Taking a deep, shaky breath, I reached for the paper airplane, my entire body tingling with anticipation. Was there a message inside? Or did he just throw it at me to be a pain? No, there had to be a message…yep, one of the wings had the words "open me" scrawled across it in black marker.

So I opened it.

He'd constructed the plane out of multiple complicated folds, and I had to admit, I was impressed, not that I knew much about the art of folding a paper airplane. Jake sure did, though. The guy was a complete mystery. One I told myself I didn't need to figure out. There was no point, considering we couldn't be involved anyway. Counselors weren't allowed to fraternize with campers, and I didn't want to get in trouble. Bobbee told me a story about a camper who got caught with a counselor a few years ago and they sent her home.

My parents would be so disappointed in me if that happened.

Maybe that was why Jake had ignored me the last two days. Because he knew we shouldn't be around each other, which hurt, but what could I do? The rules were the rules.

Though rules were always meant to be broken…

When I realized Jake was ignoring me, I stayed away because I thought it was best to keep my distance. It had proved so hard, though. I found myself staring at him every time he was nearby, always sure to look away when I thought he might catch me. He seemed to be spending a lot of time alone, which I thought was weird.

For some reason, it was like I couldn't resist Jake. It was

so strange. This whole thing started because of Kyle, but I was pretty sure I didn't like him anymore.

But Jake…oh crap, I was pretty sure I liked him.

I opened the paper and smoothed my hand over the wrinkles, not letting myself read the note yet. I wanted to draw this moment out. Instead I studied his handwriting. It was scrawled across the page, all sharp slashes and angles. I liked it. His handwriting fit him.

Finally unable to resist any longer, I started to read.

*Annie,*

*I'm sorry for being such a jerk and ignoring you. I hope you'll meet me tomorrow night at the pool at 8 so I can make up for lost time. Maybe we could even talk, and not about Kyle, either. I still owe you those last few lessons. I'm going to get you swimming by the end, I swear.*

*Yours,*
*Jake*

It took everything within me not to clutch the note to my chest and sigh like a lovesick fool. I would definitely go meet him tomorrow night. What he didn't know was that I would be at tonight's hike, too, though I probably wouldn't get a chance to talk to him.

What did he mean by "Yours, Jake," anyway? It sounded very…intimate. Boyfriend-ish even, though I was totally jumping to conclusions with that. I had no idea how to deal with that sort of thing.

Though I wanted to.

Frowning, I skimmed my fingers over the words he wrote just for me, tracing each letter, memorizing every word…

"What's it say?"

I jerked my head up to find Bobbee leaning over the back of the empty chair that sat across from me, a curious smile curling her lips. I immediately folded the note into a square and clutched it in my palm. "Um, nothing really."

"Uh-huh." She didn't believe a word I said, but I didn't need to share the note with her. It was private.

It belonged to me.

"Do you like him?" When I frowned at her, she continued, rolling her eyes. "Jake. Do you two have something going on or what?"

"No," I said vehemently, squeezing the note in my hand so tightly I could feel the sharp corners pressing into my palm. "Of course not. We're just…"

"Friends?" Bobbee supplied with raised brows. She let go of the chair and took a step back, her tone friendly but also carrying a warning. "You know Presley likes him. A lot."

I said nothing. What did it matter? I couldn't argue with her, because I knew she was right. Plus, I don't think Jake even knew Presley existed. Did that give me the tiniest glimmer of satisfaction?

Yes, not that I'd ever admit it out loud.

"And doesn't he like Lacey?" Bobbee asked.

"No," I muttered, feeling stupid for sounding—for feeling—so defensive, especially when I saw the smirk on her face.

How did the old saying go? *With friends like these, who needed enemies?* I was starting to think those words applied to the girls in my cabin, minus Kelsey, as each day passed.

And it sucked.

# Chapter Thirteen

## ANNIE

We waited on the south end of the lake, all the camper kids aged twelve and up, ready to make the annual night hike. The air was buzzing with excitement, so many people talking and laughing at the same time I could hardly make out what they were saying.

The girls in my cabin were practically bouncing up and down like hyped-up rabbits, they were so ready to start this hike. I'd heard endless stories all through dinner and as we got ready, all about the past night hikes and what happened.

"Remember when that one counselor tripped over a rock and broke his leg?" Presley had said.

"What about the time they caught those counselors making out behind a tree? Fozzie yelled at them the entire hike back to camp," Bobbee had said.

"'What about the children? Why weren't you watching the children?'" Kaycee had mimicked in her best Fozzie Bear impression before they all collapsed into fits of laughter.

Kelsey and I just looked at each other like they were crazy.

I stood with Kelsey now, trying my best to act casual but really, I was looking for Jake. Where was he? I knew he'd be here. No one could get out of the night hike, and besides, he'd told me he had to go. Fozzie Bear called out all the reinforcements to ensure he had enough staff on hand to keep the hikers in line. It was kind of insane, making the hike up the mountain with a bunch of overexcited kids in the dark.

"The best thing about the hike is jumping off the waterfall at the end," Presley said, clapping her hands. "I hope you wore your swimsuits, girls."

I did, even though there was no way I would jump off a cliff into unknown waters in the dark. I wasn't that daring or crazy. I just wore the suit to act like I would. "I'm wearing mine," I said with a faint smile.

"Me, too," Kelsey added. The moment Presley turned away, Kelsey met my gaze. "No way am I jumping into that water."

I giggled. "Me neither."

"All right, all right," Hannah yelled, waving her hands for us to gather closer to her. "We're pairing up with Brian's cabin tonight." A bunch of "ooohs" sounded, and Hannah rolled her eyes. "Pipe down, ladies. It's no big deal. As most of you know, we like to pair up a group of girls and guys, like we do every year during the night hike."

Brian's group included Kyle, and I watched nervously as they all approached, Brian sending Hannah such a scorching look it was any wonder he didn't just grab her and kiss her senseless. "Ladies," he said, his amused gaze scanning each one of us before it settled on Hannah. "Looking good this evening. Ready to conquer the mountain?"

We all let out a roar, accompanied by the much deeper roar of his cabin group. Kyle was raising his arms above his head and shouting like a gorilla along with the rest of them. He even curled his hands into fists and beat his chest.

"Fitting, since he acts like a monkey most of the time," Gwen said drolly, making me laugh.

The familiar whine of the megaphone flipping on sounded, and the loud talking settled into a dull roar.

"Okay campers, are we ready to rock this?" Fozzie Bear yelled.

A resounding *yeah!* filled the air, making Kelsey, Gwen, and me wince.

"All right then, get into your cabin pairings! We're going to then divide into two large groups and be on our way!" Fozzie said.

"Hey, new girl," a familiar voice said behind me. I turned to find Kyle standing there, a big smile on his cute face.

But I didn't get those warm fuzzies like I used to when I heard him call me new girl. And there were no butterflies fluttering in my stomach when he smiled at me, either. "Hi, Kyle," I said.

He flicked his chin at me, in that universal boy gesture-speak way they all did. "Ready for the hike?"

"Definitely."

"Going to jump off the waterfall?"

"Maybe," I hedged.

"You should. It's such a rush, especially in the dark."

"But is it safe?" Kelsey asked with a wince.

"Oh yeah," Brian said as he approached our group. "Fozzie has us go check it out and make sure it's deep enough, that the brush and debris have been cleared and that everyone can only jump from one preselected spot."

"They've been doing this for years," Hannah added. "And no one has ever hurt themselves during the jump."

"Only everywhere else," Brian said with a grin.

Their words really didn't reassure me. Not that I needed

reassuring. The jump was voluntary, and most everyone who jumped did it so they wouldn't have to hike back down the mountain. Jumping from the waterfall was the shortcut.

I'd rather hike the mountain, thanks.

"I've been assigned to your group," another familiar voice said from behind me. I glanced over my shoulder to find Jake standing there, looking beyond adorable in black swim trunks and a dark gray hoodie. "Hey, Annie."

"Hi," I said breathlessly, unable to look away from him. Okay, here came the butterflies. And that nervous, slightly scary feeling I always experienced with a crush.

As in, I was crushing on Jake. Hard.

"This looks familiar," he said, his voice low as he took a step closer to me. He reached out and tugged on the string of his hoodie that I happened to be wearing.

That I never gave back to him after that one night. I'd never washed it, either, which could be considered gross, but I rarely wore it. Besides, the soft cotton still smelled like him.

And he smelled like heaven.

"You want it back?" I asked softly.

"Nah." He shook his head, a little smile teasing the corners of his lips. "It looks better on you, anyway."

My skin went warm at his compliment.

"Hey, Fazio, why you hogging the new girl?" Kyle asked, coming to stand right beside me. "Want to partner up?" he asked, his gaze meeting mine.

"Um, sure." This was what I thought I wanted. Even better, now I seemed to have two boys fighting for my attention. My every summer camp dream come true.

But it was like the wrong boy was giving me attention, and I didn't know what to do about it. I watched helplessly as Jake gave me a grim smile before he stalked off, going over to Brian and Hannah so he could chat with them.

I watched him go, my attention on him and no one else,

and Kyle tapped me on the shoulder. "You're not hot for Fazio, are you, new girl?" he asked.

"Her name is Annie," Kelsey said, clearly irritated.

"I know that," Kyle returned, equally irritated. He turned to me. "Annie."

No butterflies. No nerves. No weak knees and hopeful thoughts. No...nothing, when I looked at Kyle.

I sneaked a glance in Jake's direction to find him watching me, too. He looked away quickly, focusing all of his attention on whatever Brian was saying, and I tore my gaze from him, smiling at Kyle and Kelsey and Gwen, who all stood in front of me with expectant expressions on their faces.

"When are we leaving?" I said, bouncing on the balls of my feet. "I'm anxious to get this going."

"Me, too," Kelsey said, glancing around like she was looking for someone, too. Hmm, interesting. "They're taking forever to do...what?"

"Who knows?" Gwen said, sounding bored. Her eyes lit up when Dane walked past. "Ah, my dream date. Think he'd jump off the waterfall with me?"

"You wish," Kyle muttered.

Gwen shot him a dirty look. "I wasn't asking you, Kyle. Besides, I'm just playing around."

That's what she always said, but we knew the truth.

I guess it was safer than pining over some boy who would hardly give you the time of day.

Or wouldn't make a move for fear of breaking the rules.

Forty-five minutes later, we were on the crest of the mountain, the view below absolutely amazing. We all stood in clusters staring at the camp spread out before us.

"Our cabin's right there," Hailey pointed out.

"Forget camp, check out the sky," Bobbee said, her head tilted back as she stared up at the stars.

"Pretty nice, huh, Annie?" Kyle asked.

"Uh-huh." He'd stuck by my side for the entire hike, helping me when my steps faltered, telling me a few crude jokes and yelling so many obscenities at his friends Brian had to threaten him twice. Jake led the group with Brian while Hannah walked behind us. Jake had never looked back at me.

Not even once.

All the girls from my cabin had shot me knowing looks throughout the hike, with the exception of Kelsey and Gwen. They both looked at me with sympathy in their eyes. Those two were too smart for their own good. They had me all figured out.

The megaphone clicked on, the whiny feedback sharp in the otherwise still night. "Who's ready to make the jump?"

Lots of squeals filled the air as dozens of campers ran toward Fozzie. He had them form two lines, and I watched as pretty much every single person from our group started heading for the line.

Kyle paused and turned to face me. "You coming, Annie?"

I shook my head and smiled weakly. "I don't think so."

"Why not?" He frowned.

"I don't like the idea of jumping into water when I can't really see it," I said.

"Me, either," Kelsey chimed in.

Kyle's frown deepened. "Seriously? It's not that big of a deal."

"It is to us," Kelsey mumbled.

"What are you guys? A couple of chickens?" Kyle practically sneered.

"Leave them alone."

I glanced over my shoulder to see Jake fast approaching us, a determined—and angry—look on his face. Relief flooded me. My knight in shining armor had run to my rescue yet again.

"I wasn't doing anything wrong—" Kyle started to say, but Jake cut him off with a shake of his head.

"Go get in line if you want to jump," he suggested, and Kyle took off to do exactly that.

"You two okay?" Jake asked once Kyle left. "Sorry if he was pushing you too hard."

"Don't apologize for him," Kelsey said. "It's not your fault he's such a jerk."

Jake smiled. "I like you."

Kelsey laughed, her cheeks turning pink. "Glad I earned your approval."

"Are you going to jump?" I asked Jake.

He shrugged, and my gaze dropped to his broad shoulders. He had really great ones. "Brian and Hannah said they'd hike back down if I wanted to, but I don't know."

I watched the line start to move, heard the first set of screams as someone jumped into the water.

"They let two people go at a time," Jake said. "Usually friends or couples or whatever."

"Maybe we should go watch for a little bit? Before we start to hike back down?" Kelsey suggested.

I nodded and started nibbling on my thumbnail, trying to calm my nerves. "Okay."

"I'll take you two over there," Jake suggested, his smile warm as his gaze met mine. "Stand guard and make sure no one tries to give you crap for not jumping."

I returned his smile, the butterflies warring big-time in my stomach at the way he was watching me. "Thanks, Jake."

"Anytime," he murmured.

• • •

## JAKE

I led the girls over so we stood close to the edge, but not too close. The roar of the water falling into the pond far below was loud, drowning out most everyone's conversations, but I didn't care what anyone else was saying.

I only cared about Annie.

"It's so far down," she said, her friend making a distressed sound of agreement.

"The pond is super deep so it's never dangerous," I reassured her, smiling when another group of two jumped off the edge, their screams loud as they went plunging down.

"There is just no possible way I could ever want to do this," Kelsey said, wrinkling her nose as she shook her head.

"Have you done it before?" Annie asked, turning those big blue eyes on me. She didn't look that scared, more curious than anything. I sort of wished she would jump, though really, she didn't know how to swim, and I wouldn't want her to totally freak out…

I nodded slowly. "I've done it a few times. My first time was when I was a camper here."

Her eyes went even wider. "Seriously?"

"Yeah. It was fun. Did it again earlier today when we were cleaning up the place." It had been a total rush. Like every other time I'd jumped off that cliff, I'd screamed all the way down like a little girl, making Brian laugh hysterically. "It's like nothing I've ever really experienced before."

"Were you ever scared?"

I decided to be completely honest with her. "Pretty much every time. It's like you step out into nothing and I can't lie, that's terrifying. But then gravity sucks you down and you're hurtling through the air. All the breath leaving you, yet you've never felt so…alive."

"And when you hit the water?"

"Cold." I smiled. "But totally worth it."

Her gaze never leaving mine, her expression awfully solemn, she murmured, "I think I want to do it."

Kelsey gasped. "You're kidding."

Annie shook her head. "I'm not."

"Annie. You don't have to do this," I said, stepping closer to her. The screams were coming at us constantly, the kids jumping one after the other. Dane had remained at the base of the waterfall, helping guide everyone out along with a few of the other junior counselors.

She nodded, looking determined. "I want to."

"You're nuts!" Kelsey yelled, and Annie flashed her a dirty look.

"I am not."

"You kinda are," I said, low enough so only she could hear.

"I'll only do it if you jump with me," she said.

My eyes widened and I popped my mouth open, not sure what I should say.

"I trust you," she added, her gaze never flinching from mine. "The only way I can do it is if you're holding my hand. I know you won't let go."

"I won't," I said. "I promise."

She smiled serenely. "Then let's do it."

After shedding our clothes and shoes, stuffing them into Kelsey's backpack, we went to go stand in line together. Kelsey went over to the group who were getting ready to leave so she'd have our stuff waiting for us after we jumped.

I couldn't believe Annie wanted to do this. Sweet, scared-of-the-water Annie.

The shorter the line got, the more nervous she became. I snatched up her hand when we were only a few spots away from being the next jumpers. Luckily enough, Uncle Bob wasn't manning the count anymore, too distracted with rounding up those who weren't jumping and preparing to lead them back down the mountain.

"Are you sure you can do this?" I asked her.

She nodded, watching as yet another pair jumped into the darkness. "I think so," she finally said. "I want to prove to myself that I can. That I'm not scared of the water, and that we've made progress together."

"You can do it," I said confidently. I was the one who started to get nervous. My heart was thumping wildly, like it wanted to burst out of my chest. And my palms were sweating.

"Annie." Hannah looked surprised when she noticed we were third in line. "You're going to jump?"

She nodded and squeezed my hand. "Yep. With Jake."

Hannah sent me a look. One I couldn't quite figure out. "Feeling brave, huh?"

Annie looked right at me. "Definitely."

When it was our turn, I could feel her hand tremble in mine. It took everything I had not to reach out and offer her a kiss for reassurance. But I didn't. I couldn't. Annie's lips were strictly off-limits.

"You two are last in line, so take your time," Hannah said gently, which I appreciated. She was totally in tune with Annie's nerves. "You've got this."

"You do," I told Annie, giving her hand a firm shake. "Whenever you're ready, I'm ready."

Annie nodded, taking a deep breath. She took a step forward, and I followed her. We were so close to the edge, one wrong move and we'd fall over, straight into the water. She turned to look at me, her eyes huge and filled with fear. "I can do this, right?"

"You can do anything you set your mind to," I whispered.

"Okay." She tugged on my hand. "Let's jump."

"On the count of three."

One…

Two…

Three!

We leaped off the edge together, Annie screaming bloody murder, our hands still linked. The wind whistled in my ears, her fingers curled tight around mine, and it was over in a flash, our bodies slicing through the water and going down, down, down…

It was dark. Pitch-black. A totally different experience compared to this afternoon's jump. I pulled on Annie's hand, tugging her toward the surface, until both of our heads popped up out of the water and she was in my arms, a trembling, giddy, and full-of-laughter mess of a girl.

A beautiful mess of a girl.

"I did it, I did it, I did it," she chanted over and over, her teeth chattering, her words slurring together. She wrapped her arms around my neck, her legs around my waist, and I held her close, my mouth pressed to her forehead, savoring the feel of her in my arms.

"You did. I can't freaking believe it," I said as I started to laugh with her.

She pulled away slightly to look up at me. "That was freaking crazy. Am I right?"

"Yeah." I brushed her wet hair away from her forehead, my gaze locked with hers. "Totally crazy. But you did it."

Her smile was huge. She looked pleased with herself. "I did. I'm proud."

"You should be. I didn't think you had it in you."

"Knowing that you were the one to jump with me, that made it easier." Her voice dropped and she slid her arms down, her hands pressed against my chest. "You never let go of my hand once."

"I promised I wouldn't."

The air buzzed between us, the water lapping against our skin, her hands skimming down my chest. *I should kiss her. I should.* I leaned my head down and she lifted her head up, her lips parting. Like she knew exactly what I wanted. No one was paying us any attention and it was so damn dark, who'd see us? No one. Absolutely no one, so this could be our little secret…

"I can't believe you jumped!" a girl's voice shouted from behind us.

Annie let go of me completely, pushing away and smiling at whoever it was. Some pain-in-the-ass girl from her cabin, no doubt. "I know, right? I can't believe it, either!"

"You don't even want to see that drop in the daylight," the girl continued. "You'd probably throw up."

Annie laughed nervously. "What's done is done, right?"

I said nothing as I watched her wade through the water with her friend, seemingly at ease as she eventually found her footing. I stayed rooted to the spot, knowing I should get out of the water and grab one of the towels that had been brought just for the occasion. But I didn't. I watched her go, my gaze lingering, my heart hammering, my mind already reliving the moment when Annie wrapped herself around me like she never wanted to let me go.

She glanced over her shoulder as she climbed out of the water, the grateful smile on her face sending a pang straight to my heart.

And I knew, without a doubt, I'd done more than just fall into the water.

I'd fallen for the girl.

# Chapter Fourteen

It was almost eight fifteen at night when I finally pushed the gate open and ran inside the pool area. I stopped, out of breath as I looked around. Worried Jake had already left, but there he was, sitting on the edge of the pool with his feet in the water, a giant smile curving his lips when he spotted me, his brown eyes sparkling.

Oh crap. He looked…way too good.

Meaning I was in big trouble.

"I didn't think you were going to make it," he said as I approached him. He leaned back and planted his hands flat on the concrete, his biceps becoming more defined with his new position.

I swallowed hard, tearing my gaze away from the perfection known as his arms and stared into his eyes. "It was kind of difficult to sneak away without anyone noticing me." Every single girl in my cabin seemed particularly interested in my whereabouts the entire day, thanks to what happened last night at the waterfall. Oh, and yesterday afternoon, when Bobbee, Hailey, and Kaycee told everyone about Jake coming to talk to me in the arts and crafts building.

They bombarded me with questions throughout the day, most of them just curious, a few of them with malicious undertones. I knew they were curious about what happened during the hike, but I wasn't telling them anything. I knew my silence drove them nuts, but I sort of didn't care.

Okay, I *really* didn't care.

"I left when we all headed for the bonfire pit," I told him.

"Ah, yeah, camp songs around the fire." He swung his legs out of the water and pushed himself to his full height, coming to stand just in front of me. I tilted my head back so I could look into his eyes, and he smiled at me. He was just so dang tall. "Sure you don't want to go back and sing a few rounds of 'Cat's in the Cradle'? We could do this another night."

"I think I could miss a night of singing." I wrinkled my nose. "I really don't like singing, anyway. I have a terrible voice."

"Really?" He seemed surprised.

I nodded. "I can't carry a tune. I sound awful when I sing. It's really horrible."

He tilted his head to the side, his gaze locked on my face, his expression so serious. "You're the only girl I've ever met who points out her own flaws."

I reared my head back, shocked by his statement. "Really? We all tend to think we're pretty flawed most of the time. Even in ways that we're not." I had about a bazillion insecurities, and so did my friends.

"Yeah, but no girl I've ever known actually points out her flaws to me. You're always the first to say what you can't do or what you're not good at."

"Oh." I winced. "Is that a bad thing?"

"I don't think so."

He said nothing else, and I didn't know how to react, what to say next. I was tempted to tackle-hug him for being kind of sweet, but that would be ridiculous. He was letting me know that I was dumb enough to point out my flaws. He wasn't saying that he thought I was amazing or anything like that.

Because I'm sure he didn't feel that way. He couldn't. Just because he wrote me a sweet note and folded it into a paper airplane didn't mean anything. Or that he was so supportive last night, how he held my hand when we jumped off the ledge. He never let go, even when we plunged into the water. At one point, I'm pretty sure he was going to kiss me.

But he didn't. Which meant I was probably reading too much into what was really nothing.

"So you ready for your swim lesson? Though I gotta say, you were pretty impressive last night, Annie. I still can't believe you did that." His words pulled me from my thoughts and I nodded, eager to get this going yet already sad that it would eventually end. After tonight's lesson, we only had one left.

I didn't even want to think about that last lesson.

Jake smiled. "Then let's do this. We'll start in the shallow end."

I followed after him, settling on the edge beside him, both of us dunking our feet into the water. I sat closer to him this time, our arms brushing, and he looked over at me, his gaze dropping to my chest. "You should take off your shirt." He literally said this to my boobs.

My cheeks went instantly hot and I socked him in the upper arm, shocked at how hard it was. His biceps were nothing but solid muscle. And what he just said could be taken so many ways. What did it mean that my brain filled with dirty thoughts?

He laughed, like he could read my mind. "I only said that because we're going to get in the water like, right now."

"Right," I said, laughing along with him. "I think I'll wait."

"Your choice." He shrugged, the laughter dying on his lips before he said, his voice soft, "Tell me what happened to you when you were four, Annie."

I sat up straighter, all dirty thoughts fleeing my brain like they were being chased out. And they were, because I had a flash of memory. Of the water sucking me under, of me struggling.

Of feeling like I was dying.

"You can trust me with your secret, I promise. I won't tell anyone else." His voice was gentle, as were his eyes, and I pressed my lips together, not wanting to talk about it. It wasn't a subject I was comfortable sharing, only because I hadn't talked about the incident in so long. I'd rather forget it ever happened.

"How about I tell you something that I've never told anyone else first," he suggested.

I raised my brows, surprised by his offer. "Like what?"

He looked down, staring at the water. "My mom died three years ago, when I was fourteen. She had cancer. It came…really fast so she didn't suffer for too long or anything like that, but it was so quick that it felt like one day she was there, and the next, she was just…gone."

"I'm so sorry," I automatically said, feeling awful. I couldn't imagine losing my parents. I don't know what I would do, how I would react.

"You don't have to apologize. It was just…it was hard. I was scared and mad. Mad at my mom for leaving me, though she didn't have a choice. I was just really confused. My dad retreated. He didn't want to talk about it, or talk about her. He acted like he wanted to just move on and pretend she never existed."

"That sounds awful," I said softly.

"It was. He didn't know how to mourn, I think. It suddenly

became the two of us on our own, and we didn't realize what she did for us until she was gone, you know? He was never around. He became a complete workaholic, and I spent a lot of time alone." Jake hesitated. "And eventually I got…into a lot of trouble."

I remembered the rumors I heard about him being a criminal, and how Presley had declared him even hotter when she heard that bit of gossip. I hadn't believed the criminal stories at the time, and he'd been so sweet to me I hadn't thought much about the rumors since, but here was Jake confirming everything. "Oh," I murmured, not sure what else I could say.

"Like, throw me in juvie, threaten me with jail and probation type trouble." He turned to look at me, his expression serious, his eyes dark as he watched me. "I just wanted you to know the truth. In case that changed your mind about me."

I frowned. "Why would it change my mind about you?"

"I don't know. We had a rocky start, you gotta admit that," he said wryly, his lips tipping up at the corners in an almost-smile. "I wanted you to find out all my dirty secrets from me, not from someone else."

"Oh," I said again, at a loss for words. That my opinion of him mattered so much made me feel fluttery inside. "Well, I appreciate that."

"I just wanted to be up front with you."

"Do you still do those things? Whatever it was you did that got you in trouble?"

He looked away, squinting as he watched the darkening sky. "Not in a while. I'm under constant watch by my uncle. That's why I'm here, actually. My dad didn't know what else to do with me."

His admission made my heart ache. Did he feel unwanted? If my parents shipped me off to camp because they didn't know what else to do with me, I think I'd feel that way. At least he had his uncle here, but they didn't seem that close. Now that he'd mentioned it, I never really saw him hanging out with friends or anything like that. Not really. He worked all the time.

I'd seen him with Dane and knew they shared one of the staff cabins. At first he was hanging out with Kyle, but they weren't around each other much anymore. He and Brian were friendly, too, but Brian had been spending all of his free time with Hannah lately—trust me, everyone in our cabin knew this, since Hannah left pretty much every night to be with Brian.

Did Jake have any real friends here? I didn't want to ask because I didn't want to embarrass him. So I tried a different tactic. "Do you like working here?"

He shrugged and looked away again. "I guess. I don't know. I feel like I'm being forced to do this, so my heart's not fully in it, you know?"

"Yeah, I know. The summer is almost over, but maybe you should try. It's not so bad here. And everyone likes you." I leaned into him and nudged his shoulder with mine. "We should get the swimming lesson started."

He glanced down at where our shoulders were still pressed together before lifting his gaze to mine. "You still want to go through with this?"

"Of course I do. I have to work on it so I can get enough courage to actually hang out at the pool with my friends and maybe even really swim." At his doubtful look I added, "Or at the very least, I could become a really good doggy-paddler."

I smiled and he chuckled, and for the briefest moment, with us sitting so close, our shoulders brushing, the both of us breathing the same air, I thought he might…I don't know.

Try to kiss me again?

But he didn't. I don't know if it was relief or disappointment

I felt, but he stood, offering his hand to me, and I took it so he could pull me up, my fingers tingling in his grip. He let go as soon as I stood, and I fought the wave of disappointment that threatened. I was being ridiculous. I shouldn't like Jake in that way. We were friends. That was it. That was all we could be.

"Let's jump in the shallow end and work on your kicks some more," he suggested, taking his hat off and tossing it on a nearby chair.

I could do nothing but agree.

• • •

## JAKE

This was pure torture, spending time with Annie, trying to focus on giving her instructions and encouragement when all I really wanted to do was kiss her for being so understanding about my mom's death. Oh, and stare at her ass in those bright pink bikini bottoms. Maybe even touch that ass in those bright pink bikini bottoms...

Yeah. Couldn't do it. Couldn't touch. Shouldn't even think about it. I scrubbed a hand over my face and told her to turn around so she was facing me, her arms stretched out behind her as she still gripped the concrete edge of the pool, her chest bobbing above the water, giving me a perfect view of her...

I closed my eyes and turned my back on her, dunking under the water to cool myself off as I swam all the way to the deep end before I turned around and swam back. By the time I popped my head out of the water, she was standing, clapping her hands and with a big smile on her face.

"You are such a good swimmer," she said, her voice wistful.

"Dunk your head underwater and you'll be halfway there," I tell her.

Her smile fell and fear filled her eyes. "I don't think I'm

ready for that yet," she admitted in a whisper.

"You did it last night," I pointed out. "When you jumped in the water with me. And you did it that night I saved you at the dock, too."

"That was different." She ducked her head, suddenly shy. I didn't get her. She'd been so bold last night. I'd been so proud of her, she'd looked so pretty, I'd come scarily close to kissing her in front of freaking everyone.

But I hadn't. I'd been the chicken last night while she'd been the brave one.

"Find some of that courage you had last night and use it right now," I suggested, but she shook her head, remaining quiet.

"Annie. The only way you're going to feel comfortable in the water is if you completely submerge yourself in it. Like you did last night," I told her, trying to keep my voice gentle. I didn't want to yell or sound too demanding, but the girl needed some major encouragement. I knew that so much of her fear was mental, even if she hadn't told me the story of why. And though I'd just spilled my guts, I hadn't pushed. She'd reveal everything when she was ready. And maybe then, we'd have a breakthrough.

For now, it was all baby steps, pretty much all the time. I'd never been the most patient person, but for Annie, I'd try.

She shook her head. "No."

"Why not?"

"It scares me."

"Do you take a shower?"

She frowned. "Of course I do."

"How often?"

"Why such a sudden interest in my personal hygiene?"

"Just answer the question."

"Once a day at least, sometimes twice." She stared at me incredulously.

"You stick your face in the water every time you take a shower, right?"

Realization dawned and she scowled. "That's totally different."

"Not really."

She sighed and pushed away from the ledge, wading closer to me. "Fine, you want to see me stick my face in the water?"

"I'd frickin' *love* to see you stick your face in the water," I practically taunted.

Annie waded closer as I floated out farther. She frowned as she followed me, getting chest deep before she stopped, her face so close to the water I thought she really was going to do it.

She took such a deep breath I could see the gust of air ripple the water directly in front of her when she slowly exhaled. Her head bent, she closed her eyes, pressed her lips together, and actually...

Dipped her face in the water.

Her head immediately popped back up, her eyes still squeezed shut as she let out a shuddery sob. I rushed toward her, slicing through the water until I had her in my arms, her head tucked under mine and her face pressed against my chest. "Shit, Annie. You didn't have to do that," I muttered as I felt her body quake. She was crying. I could hear the hiccuping breaths, the little sniffles in between, and I felt like a complete asshole for pushing her so hard.

I didn't understand why she'd jumped into the water last night, yet tonight, she couldn't even duck her head in the pool. We were safer here, right now, than we ever were last night.

"I'm just so tired of being scared," she whispered, her lips moving across my skin when she spoke, and I shivered because wow, even though she was sad and crying and a trembling mess in my arms, that brief touch of her mouth on me felt good.

Too good.

She looped her arms around my neck and clung to me, crying into my shoulder, and I just let her. Smoothed my hand over her hair, an all-out war happening within me as I wondered if I should touch her anywhere else. We were standing in the middle of the pool completely wrapped around each other, so much skin making actual contact, and here I was, almost afraid to touch her.

"Don't cry," I said helplessly. It felt like she would never stop. I wasn't used to crying girls, and I didn't know how to deal or how to make her feel better. Her tears were breaking my heart, and I'd firmly believed I didn't have one anymore after I lost my mom.

"I'm sorry," she said with a sniff, lifting her head away from my shoulder so she could look up at me. Her arms were still around my neck, her fingers absently playing with the ends of my hair, and I lifted one shoulder, trying to ease the shivery feeling her touch was causing. "I didn't mean to fall apart like that."

"I think you pushed yourself too hard." I'd helped with that, too, not that I wanted to admit it.

"Totally." She sniffed and smiled up at me even through the tears. "You were kind of a jerk."

"I was going for encouraging, but I don't think it worked," I admitted.

"It's okay," she said softly. "Really. I'm not mad. More like disappointed in myself."

She dropped her arms from my neck, and I immediately felt empty. I slowly pushed away from her, and we both headed toward the shallow end, neither of us saying anything. My brain felt like a tornado had blown straight through it, twisting my thoughts into a confused, jumbled mess.

How did I feel about her? How did she feel about me?

Crap, was she still hot for that stupid tool Kyle? I really didn't think so, not anymore, though I still worried. Worried more that she thought of me as that annoying guy who owed her a few swim lessons.

I didn't know. And I didn't know how to ask her, either. I was just left questioning everything.

After tonight's swim lesson, I was more confused than ever.

# Chapter Fifteen

JAKE

"So come on, tell me the truth. You like the new girl, don't you?" Brian asked conversationally as we were gathering wood for that night's bonfire.

I stopped tossing a few logs into the wheelbarrow beside me, wiping the sweat off my forehead with my wrist, since my hands were covered with work gloves to prevent splinters from getting into my skin. "I'm pleading the fifth."

"What? Get the hell out. Just admit it." Brian tossed a bundle of kindling in his wheelbarrow and glanced around before he returned his gaze to me. "No one else is nearby. Your secret is safe with me."

Should I trust him? We weren't that close—not because we didn't like each other, but because he chose to spend all of his free time with Hannah. I understood why, too. They were totally into each other. Hannah was cute and nice, and she seemed like fun. They made a good couple. I could even admit I was sort of envious of what they shared.

"Yeah," I reluctantly admitted. "I like her. But I can't do anything about it because of the rules. And my uncle really holds me to them, too."

Brian made an irritated face. "Screw the rules, man. Everyone pairs up around here all the time, especially the junior counselors and the last-year campers. What are you, seventeen?"

I nodded and grabbed my water bottle, taking a long swig. It was hot as hell out here today, and we were doing manual labor under the blazing sun. I couldn't wait to get back to the lake so I could jump in and cool off before I resumed lifeguard duty.

"And she's gotta be what? Sixteen?"

"I've never asked her," I said after I took another drink. Maybe I should. Crap, what if she was fifteen or...fourteen? Fourteen was practically a freakin' baby.

"She's with the last-year bunk, so she has to be sixteen. Don't get your panties in a twist. She's not some tween you're fantasizing about." Brian laughed and shook his head. "I mean, seriously, what's the big deal if you two wanted to hang out? How's that a crime? I'll even let you in on my own secret." He took a few steps closer, like he was going to share something particularly juicy. "Last year, Hannah and I hooked up."

"So?"

"So I was a nineteen-year-old counselor who'd just finished with my freshman year of college and Hannah was sixteen and only done with her junior year in high school." I raised my eyebrows and he laughed. "But who gives a shit? I thought she was cute, she was into me, so yeah. We started hanging out and I really got to know her. We liked each other. When the summer was over, we went our separate ways but still kept in contact, you know?"

"Really?"

He nodded, looking sheepish. "I went and saw her during

part of winter break, just before Christmas. Stayed the week at her parents' house and had to sleep in her older brother's room, since he'd moved out the year before last. It was kind of weird. Her parents didn't know what to think of us."

"Wow, you two were really trying to make this work." I was surprised. I never thought much of these camp relationships. Always figured they were brief flings before the summer was over.

"We're in love," he admitted. "She graduated from high school in June, and she's going to UNC with me in the fall."

"Seriously? Are you guys moving in together?" I asked.

"Nah, she's living in the dorms while I'm off campus, but we're definitely serious about each other." Brian slipped off his work gloves and stretched his fingers out. "I'm just trying to tell you that if you really like this girl, don't let that stupid rule get in the way. You're only a year apart. It's no big deal. You can either go your separate ways at the end of summer, or you can stay in contact and see if you could really make this work."

Huh. Who knew Brian was such a romantic, or that he and Hannah had such a serious relationship? They were in love. They were going to the same college together. It sort of blew my mind, but then again, if you cared about someone — really *loved* someone, you'd do whatever it took to be together.

I didn't know if I'd ever be capable of loving someone. I had my own issues I really hadn't dealt with and still wasn't sure if I wanted to. Like the death of my mother and the loss of the dad I once had. He wasn't the same person any longer, but neither was I. We hadn't been getting along for years. He'd threatened me more than once that he would kick me out of the house if I didn't get my act together. And I'd countered by threatening to run away. It was a threat we made a lot and we knew we didn't mean it, which meant they were both empty threats. So stupid.

So pointless.

We were a mess, my dad and I. Maybe he'd been right all along, and coming here for the summer really was a good thing. We needed to spend some time apart. I could even admit I sort of missed him.

I should call him later, from the office phone, see if he was missing me, too. Uncle Bob would let me. I should invite Dad to come see me for the weekend, though I don't know if he could, what with his work schedule. At the very least, it would be good to hear his voice.

"It's ghost story night," Brian told me as he slipped back on his work gloves and we both grabbed our wheelbarrows, redirecting ourselves so we were headed back to the bonfire pit. "And we have a special guest."

"What are you talking about?" I followed along beside him, doing my best to avoid the ruts in the trail.

"It's pretty cool, actually. Nancy from arts and crafts will dress up like some creepy old lady. Like, she becomes totally unrecognizable with the makeup she puts on, plus the costume and the wig. Anyway, she sits in a special rocking chair we only bust out once a year and tells these super-creepy stories that freaks everyone's shit out. The younger kids aren't allowed to participate, since Nancy really lays on the scary drama, and they'd be out of their damn minds, but everyone else loves it." Brian smiled. "It'll be a perfect opportunity for you to get close to your girl and offer her some comfort in her time of frightened need."

I started to laugh at Brian's choice words. "You've got this all figured out, don't you?"

"Dude, I spent all of last summer trying to figure out ways to get Hannah alone. Even if we weren't totally one-on-one, I was plotting how I could hold her hand, touch her somehow without anyone noticing. I've got it down to a fine-tuned skill, let me tell you."

What he said hung in my mind long after we went our separate ways. I was headed toward the lake, thinking of the many different scenarios that could happen tonight between Annie and me. I could wrap my arm around her shoulders, tuck her close to my side. Or maybe hold her hand to calm her down. I could hug her. I could let her press her face against my chest. Hell, I could kiss her, too, if that was what she really wanted.

I'd do just about anything she wanted me to. I was sick of worrying about what would happen if we got caught. I was too caught up in Annie to worry about anything else.

I was so wrapped up in my thoughts I didn't notice the girl who was coming at me full speed from the opposite side of the trail. She practically ran straight into me without stopping, and I reached out to grab her, holding her in place.

"Jake! Just the man I'm looking for." She bounced away from me, her smile wide, her long, wavy, dark blond hair swinging past her shoulders. She was cute, with bright blue eyes and a great smile, but she wasn't as pretty as Annie. I recognized her immediately, though I didn't know her name. She was one of the girls from Annie's cabin, so what would she want from me?

"What's up, ahh…?" My mind drew a complete blank.

"Presley," she filled in for me.

"Yeah, Presley. Why are you looking for me?"

"Well, I wanted to ask you a question." She looked up at me, her expression pure innocence. I knew I couldn't trust her. "I was hoping you'd sit with me at the bonfire tonight. The ghost stories are supposed to be extra spooky," she added as a temptation.

Huh. This girl was playing dirty. She had to know Annie and I had a little something going on, even if we hadn't properly confirmed it. Yet she had no problem basically asking me out.

"Uh, I'm sorry, but no can do," I said as gently as I could. "I have to work tonight."

Her face fell a little, though that smile of hers never really faltered. "Oh, I can help you!"

"Fozzie Bear doesn't like it when the campers mess with fire. It's against camp policy. Only counselors can help set and maintain the fire."

"Aw, well maybe some other time, then?" she asked.

"Maybe," I said, though I didn't mean it. I had no plans to ever spend any one-on-one time with her.

I was hoping to save that all for Annie.

"Okay, see you around." She leaped forward and before I could stop her, before I could even utter a word of protest, she pressed a kiss to my cheek and then bounded away. I stood watching her go, too in shock that she pulled something like that, but how mad could I be? It was just a stupid kiss on the cheek.

It meant absolutely nothing.

. . .

## ANNIE

"Tonight ought to be interesting," Gwen said as she bent closer to the mirror, carefully applying black liquid eyeliner to her eyelid. No one could do a cat eye like Gwen.

"Why do you say that?" I stood next to her in front of the mirror. We were getting ready before dinner. I didn't put on much makeup because I was an utter fail at applying it compared to the rest of the girls in my cabin, but I could manage a little eyeliner and some mascara.

Gwen stood up straight, her gaze meeting mine as I did the same. "It's our annual special edition ghost story night, when Nancy dresses up as a creepy old lady and tells even creepier ghost stories."

"Sounds fun."

"It definitely is." Gwen capped her liquid eyeliner and threw it into her makeup bag. "The stories are so scary, it's when most of the guys take advantage of getting a girl to sit close to them. Offer them comfort, so to speak."

I thought of who I'd want to sit next to if I was extra scared—and it wasn't Kyle anymore.

It was Jake.

"It's basically the only time we can make out in front of everyone and we won't get in trouble," Gwen added sarcastically before she started to laugh. "It's a total hookup night."

"Oh, well." I smiled helplessly, wishing I had something interesting to say, but I was at a total loss for words. All I could think about was Jake. Sitting with him in the back of the group, where all the older kids hung out. Squeezing his hand tight when I got scared. Feeling his arm sneak around my shoulders as he pulled me close to him. Our lips meeting in our first kiss…

My first kiss. I could only imagine what it might feel like. I'd read enough books, seen plenty of on-screen kisses that looked amazing. I wanted amazing. I wanted my first kiss to be with someone special.

"Who do you want to hook up with tonight?" Gwen asked, her expression curious. "Kyle?"

My heart sank. Not even close, but how could I admit that? I didn't want them to know I liked Jake. I didn't want to hear their warnings about how I shouldn't be involved with a counselor. I knew it was wrong, yet I didn't care. But I didn't want everyone to think I still had a crush on Kyle, either.

I didn't know what to say or how to answer.

"Guess what!" Presley screeched as she ran into the bathroom, her body practically vibrating with excitement.

Gwen sent me a look like she thought Presley was crazy before she turned to her. "What, Pres?"

"I just ran into Jake, like, literally." Presley giggled as my heart felt like it was sinking even lower. Why was she talking about my Jake? "Out by the lake. We talked for a while. God, he's so cute!"

I could say nothing, couldn't even find my voice. It was like it disappeared.

"What did you talk about?" Gwen asked.

"Just dumb stuff. Then I asked him if he'd sit with me tonight." Presley grinned, looking very pleased with herself.

"And what did he say?" Gwen shot me a look, and I tried my best to keep my expression neutral. I had a feeling she was onto me, but I wasn't about to say anything.

"Oh, well, that was the disappointing part. He said he couldn't sit with me, since he had to work. He's in charge of the bonfire," Presley explained, like she was imparting secret Jake knowledge to us.

"That's too bad," Gwen said.

"Yeah," I added, my voice scratchy. I cleared my throat.

"Oh, hey. Annie." Presley turned toward me. "You two are friends, right? You and Jake?"

That's what I'd told them when they kept questioning me about the arts and crafts paper airplane incident. And the jumping into the waterfall incident. Jake and I were racking up all sorts of incidents, weren't we? I shrugged, trying to act casual. "Sort of."

"Maybe you could put in a good word for me. Like I did for you with Kyle." Presley beamed.

"Wait, what? You talked to Kyle about me?" Dread slithered down my spine, making me cold. At the beginning of the session, I would have been thrilled, but now I was almost scared of what she had to say.

"Oh, yeah. He's interested." Presley sent me a sly look, her lips pursed. "Said he's sick of the same girls every summer. You're like a breath of fresh air."

"He actually said that?" Gwen started to laugh. "I find that hard to believe."

"He did, I swear." Presley waved a hand, dismissing Gwen. "Whatever. It's true, Annie. Don't be surprised if he sits with you tonight. And if anything happens, just remember who you have to thank." She laughed and started to leave the bathroom, calling over her shoulder, "Me!"

I resumed my position in front of the mirror, trying to apply mascara with a shaky hand and nearly stabbing my eye with the stupid wand. I set the tube on the sink and exhaled loudly.

"Nervous about what Presley did by talking to Kyle?" Gwen shrugged. "She's relatively harmless. But let me say something up front—no way did Kyle call you a breath of fresh air."

"Why would you think that?" Her remark stung. Why *wouldn't* Kyle say that? Was she jealous? Did she wish Kyle said that about her instead?

"Because Kyle doesn't say stuff like that. Honestly?" Her gaze met mine in the mirror's reflection, her expression serious. "Kyle's not the...*smartest* guy I know."

Great. Now was she bashing Kyle? "You really shouldn't make fun of him, Gwen."

"I'm not!" She shook her head, looking exasperated. "I'm actually trying to tell you something, friend to friend." Her voice lowered. "Seriously, he's as dumb as a rock, Annie. You're like, a thousand times smarter than him. You could do so much better. Trust me."

Gwen zipped up her cosmetics bag and smiled softly at me. "Don't take too long. We're leaving for dinner in a few minutes." And with that, she walked out of the bathroom.

Her words rang in my head as I finished applying my mascara with a steadier hand. Maybe Gwen was being serious by letting me know her opinion of Kyle. Maybe she was trying to be a good friend and warn me.

We left for dinner a few minutes later, everyone chatting nonstop as we walked toward the dining hall with the exception of me. I'd been on meal detail all day, meaning I was the one who had to go pick up dinner for my table. I was actually looking forward to it. It meant I could get away from the girls for a little bit and their endless gossiping about the boys at camp.

"Tonight is important," Bobbee said with all the authority of a girl who'd been coming to this camp for over a decade. "Whatever boy you end up with tonight is usually the one you spend the rest of the summer with, even though there's not much time left. As in, he's the boy who asks you to next week's dance."

I frowned. There was a dance? Oh God. Just thinking about it made my stomach feel like it was full of a hundred buzzing, angry bees.

"What if you don't end up with any boy?" Kelsey asked, sounding worried. Not that I could blame her. She hadn't shown even a hint of interest in any guy, and all of the other girls thought she was kind of weird. Not that they'd ever say that to her face, but I heard their whispers. They talked about her behind her back. They talked about one another behind their backs.

I'm sure they'd talked about me, too.

"Then you're doomed to spend the rest of the summer alone," Kaycee announced, making everyone laugh, except for Kelsey.

Except for me.

We entered the dining hall, and the girls sat at a table while I went over to start collecting our dinner. It was a simple one tonight—hamburgers and fries—and I ignored the silverware, thankful I wouldn't have to carry as much back to the table.

"Hey, Annie."

I glanced to my left to see—oh crap—Kyle standing next to me, a tentative smile on his face. He looked nervous.

And I immediately felt nervous. "Hi, Kyle."

"What are you doing?"

"Um, getting dinner?" Fairly obvious, right? Gwen's earlier words rang clear in my head.

I pushed them to the back of my brain, trying to ignore them.

"Right." He laughed. Shrugged. Looked around. Shoved his hands into the front pockets of his shorts. "So are you going to be around later tonight? During the ghost stories?"

My heart thumped erratically against my ribs, and my mouth went dry. Did Presley really talk to him about me after all? This was my chance. The opportunity I'd been waiting for since the day I got here.

So why was I tempted to say no? Tempted to run away from him and pretend like he never talked to me?

"Annie?" He prompted when I still hadn't said anything.

I shook myself and smiled at him. "Um, yeah. I'll be there tonight."

"Dope. I'll see you later, then." He turned and walked back to his table completely empty-handed.

Like the only reason he'd been there was to talk to me.

I didn't know what to think, how to react. I glanced over at my table to see all seven heads watching me, their smiles huge, their eyes sparkling as they started to make all sorts of lovey, kissy gestures. Turning away, I scanned the entire room, my gaze settling on Jake and where he sat with the rest of the miscellaneous staff.

He was watching me, his expression dark, his mouth thin. Like he just saw everything go down between Kyle and me, and he didn't like it. Jake bent his head, tearing his gaze from mine.

And it felt like he just tore a hole in my heart.

# Chapter Sixteen

### JAKE

I was angry and I had no reason to be, not really. So Kyle talked to her. So what? She never laughed when he talked to her. She didn't blush, either. I took that as a good sign. Maybe I was the only one who could make her laugh, could make her cheeks turn pink. I liked it when she blushed. It was cute. Everything about her was cute.

Pretty.

Beautiful.

Ah, crap, I had it frickin' bad.

Grabbing another piece of wood out of the wheelbarrow, I threw it into the fire, the flames snapping and little sparks flying high into the night sky. Brian started to laugh, and I shot him a dirty look, which shut him up.

"What's your prob tonight?" Brian asked.

I didn't answer him. Supposedly this night wasn't just about Nancy telling trippy ghost stories in the hopes of giving us all massive nightmares. It was also a night when everyone who'd been circling each other the last few weeks finally tried to seal the deal. And by seal the deal, that meant they made out, declared each other boyfriend and girlfriend or whatever other bullshit they wanted to do to further their romantic lives.

It all sounded like a bunch of crap to me. Especially when I saw that tool Kyle go talk to Annie during dinner. He had a plan for her tonight, I could tell. When he returned to his table, all the other guys had given him a high five. He wanted to hook up with Annie.

My Annie.

Frowning, I told myself I couldn't be that possessive. She didn't belong to me. I was still so confused I didn't know exactly how she felt about me. We could consider each other friends. We'd grown closer. But was she interested in me beyond being a friend? Having her in my arms last night in the pool, that wasn't just a friendly hug. That had been more.

But maybe it had only been more to me. Maybe she thought nothing of it. Nothing of me.

She was too good for me anyway.

I grabbed another log and threw it into the fire, making Brian yell, "Watch out, dude!"

Screw it. I was pissed and taking it out on the fire.

"Go sit down and cool off," Brian said, waving toward the old log benches that surrounded the bonfire area. "You're going to set this whole place on fire if you don't calm down."

Yeah. I felt like I could burn the entire camp down with my anger alone, which was so freaking stupid. I was trying to get that shit under control. Not let things get to me anymore. I'd been doing so well, too. Teaching the kids at swim lessons in the morning, working my lifeguard detail with no complaints and even earning a few compliments from Dane lately. Hell, I had Nancy approach me this morning asking if I'd lead a paper-airplane-making class in arts and crafts next week. I'd said yes, too stunned by her request to say anything else.

But now I was acting like a jealous fool, all because I saw Kyle talk to Annie. Who knew what he said to her? I could be mad over nothing. Though I doubted it. Kyle was interested in Annie. Annie was interested in Kyle. Her dreams were finally coming true. I should be happy for her.

I wasn't.

"I'll be back in a minute," I told Brian before I jogged over to the main building, where Uncle Bob's office was. I walked inside, smiling at his secretary as I went past her desk. The woman worked morning, noon, and night. It was like she never took any time off. I bet she slept at her desk, too.

Knocking on Uncle Bob's partially open door, I heard him yell "come in," and I pushed the door open to find him sitting behind his desk. Leaning back in his chair, his feet kicked up on the desk, his arms bent behind his head. He looked like he was taking a nap.

"Ah, I was just headed out to the fire now. Can't wait to see what Nancy has up her sleeve tonight." He pushed his feet off the desk and sat forward, a big grin on his face. "What are you up to, Jake?"

"Could I use the phone? I want to call my dad." He'd been on my mind a lot lately, especially after my conversation with Annie last night, and I was seized with the need to call him. Maybe not the best idea, considering I still had residual anger coursing through my veins, but maybe hearing his voice would calm me down. Remind me why I was really here.

To get my head on straight, not let it get fucked with by some girl.

"Of course you can call your dad. I'm leaving right now, so you can have some privacy." Uncle Bob waved a hand toward the phone that sat on his desk. "Don't talk too long, though. You don't want to miss Nancy's stories!"

He rose from his chair, and I watched him lumber across

his office. Stopping at the door, he turned to look at me. "Tell your dad I said hello." They were brothers, but they weren't that close anymore. My dad had distanced himself from everyone after Mom died.

"I will," I said, settling in Bob's just vacated chair. "Thanks, Uncle Bob."

"Of course. And like I said, don't talk too long. I've been waiting to hear Nancy's scary ghost stories all year. They're the best." He shut the door behind him and was gone.

Great. So Uncle Bob would be there tonight. I knew it would end up a make-out fest, but I didn't want him to see me with Annie.

If I even had a chance to get with Annie tonight.

Feeling miserable, I dialed my dad's number, grateful when he answered on the second ring.

"Hey Dad. It's me."

"Jacob! How are you? Everything okay?" We'd had a deal that I wouldn't call much this summer. We were both fine with that at the time. He'd been frustrated with me and I'd been resentful toward him, so it worked out.

But for some reason, it felt good to hear his voice.

"I'm fine," I said, pushing past the crack of emotion I heard in my voice. I hoped he didn't notice. "I just wanted to call and say hey. So…hey."

"Hey. How's the weather up there?"

"Hot. Muggy."

"Breathing in all that mountain air has to be good for you."

"Yeah, I guess so. I spend most of my time outside, since I'm a lifeguard." He already knew that, but I thought I'd remind him.

"Making friends?"

I rolled my eyes. He sounded like I was a ten-year-old camper, not a counselor. "I guess."

"Met any girls?"

"Sort of." Now the conversation had become flat-out awkward.

"Some of my fondest memories are of the girls I met during summer camp."

"Are you serious? I didn't know you went to camp."

"I went to the very camp you're at," he admitted. "So did your uncle. Seems like he loved it way more than I ever did. That's why he's still there."

We never talked about the past, Dad and I. He didn't like to focus on it, or so I thought. "What sort of girls did you meet at camp?"

"Well, I ended up a junior counselor there one summer and…I met your mother."

"Seriously?" My voice cracked. Again. I had no idea they met here.

"Seriously. She was the prettiest girl I'd ever seen. I knew the moment I laid eyes on her that I needed to spend the entire summer with her. So I did. Once we got to know each other, we found out we lived in the same town and that was that. We were together." He laughed, sounding…happy? I couldn't remember the last time he sounded like this. "It was like we were meant to be."

It hurt, to hear him talk about her. To hear that wistful tone in his voice, the love that he felt for her. A lump formed in my throat, and I tried to swallow past it. I needed to change the subject.

"There's this girl," I said. "This is her first year here, and she's just so…" What? I couldn't describe Annie with just a few simple words. There were so many things I could say about her. That she was scared yet strong. That she was determined and smart and had no fear of telling me how she really felt. It was like she understood me, that I understood her, and I'd never been so comfortable with a girl before. Not like how I felt when I was with Annie.

But I didn't want to look like a sap, not even in front of my father. "I like her," I said instead.

"If she's a camper, then you're not supposed to get involved with her, right? Since you're a counselor." He sounded worried. He sounded more like my dad.

Just great. I should've never brought her up.

"Right. I haven't done anything, I promise." I didn't want him mad. And I definitely didn't want him telling Uncle Bob that I had feelings for a camper. Next thing I knew, I'd be in trouble.

Though I was surprised my dad wasn't as mad as I figured he'd be.

"Good. Keep on the straight and narrow." I rolled my eyes at his words. "Do the right thing, son. I trust that you're able to figure out what that is."

We ended the call, and I remained in Uncle Bob's chair for a few quiet minutes, going over everything my dad said.

Yeah. I wanted to do the right thing. But I also wanted Annie. When did I ever really follow the rules?

Though this time, I should. I didn't want to get fired. Kicked out of camp, sent back home. Everything would be over for me. I'd be in juvie; I might even get kicked out of school.

Doing the right thing was boring. I went after what I wanted, rules be damned. As long as I was careful, we wouldn't get caught.

And I was always careful.

· · ·

## ANNIE

My group arrived at the bonfire site a few minutes before the ghost stories were scheduled to start. The place was already packed, so many people paired off into couples, and I glanced around, looking for Jake.

Instead, I spotted Kyle first, who approached me with a big smile on his handsome face. I could admit he looked really good tonight, wearing a blue button-up shirt and black shorts, his hair actually combed back. "Hey, you made it," he said in greeting.

"Yeah. I did." Of course I did. I told him I'd be here. Though I guess something could've happened to me in between dinner and now. Or I could've decided to ditch tonight. Kelsey had. I didn't know where she ran off to, but she'd asked me to cover for her after dinner and I'd automatically said yes.

She'd become more and more mysterious lately, and I had no idea what she was up to.

"Dope." He nodded, glanced around, seeming uncomfortable. It felt like a lot of people were watching us, which was weird. "So, uh. You wanna sit together?"

Two weeks ago I would've died for this opportunity. I wouldn't have even hesitated a second to say yes. I should probably say yes, because this was, after all, Kyle. The boy I crushed on. The boy I was learning to swim for. The boy I declared to my heart that I wanted. These were my summer dreams coming to fruition, and we were more than halfway through the session. We had ten days left, and finally everything was falling into place.

Yet here I stood full of doubt, my gaze darting everywhere, searching the crowd and looking for the boy who meant so much to me. More than this boy standing in front of me ever would.

But Jake was nowhere to be found. And the disappointment crashing through me at his not being here was a truth I needed to face.

I wasn't interested in Kyle. Not anymore. I wanted Jake.

"I appreciate the offer but...I sort of want to sit with

someone else," I said gently, feeling like a jerk. But it was better to be honest with him, right?

"Really? Um, all right." He glanced down, shoving his hands into his pockets, clearly uncomfortable. "I get it."

"You do?"

"Well, yeah." He looked up, his gaze meeting mine. "You're the pretty new girl. You have your choice of any guy here."

His words left me stunned. He thought I was the *pretty new girl* and had my choice of *any* guy at camp? He had to be kidding.

"Maybe I'll go ask Presley," Kyle continued. "I haven't kissed her since the summer we were eleven."

"I think that's a…good idea," I said, trying my hardest not to laugh. If he was making his girlfriend choice based on the fact it had been a while since he kissed her, then maybe I dodged a bullet.

And that would also help distract her from her supposed crush on Jake…

I went to where the rest of the girls from my cabin were sitting. We'd lost a few to boys already, and I was sure we'd lose a few more before the night was over.

"What just happened with you and Kyle, Annie? Why aren't you two sitting together? He didn't say something stupid, did he?" Bobbee reached out and touched my arm. "Kyle's such a jerk. Are you okay?"

The concern I saw in her eyes surprised me. I always thought Bobbee didn't really like me. "I'm fine," I reassured her. "Really. Kyle and I…we would never work." I decided not to tell her that I was the one who rejected Kyle first.

"I agree." Gwen was sitting on my other side and she leaned in, murmuring close to my ear. "You're better off without him."

I smiled at her. I knew she meant that in the most genuine

way possible. "Thanks, Gwen."

Fozzie Bear suddenly made his appearance, standing next to the roaring bonfire, his megaphone clutched in his hand. He flicked the power on and the thing squealed, making all of us cover our ears.

We all hated that thing as much as he loved it.

"Who's ready to hear some spooky stories?"

A chorus of "me!" rose up into the air.

"Good, good! Sounds like we're ready! So let's get this party started!" he announced.

Perfect. I was ready to start, too. Maybe I wouldn't sit with the boy of my choice tonight, but I was with my friends.

And that would be good enough.

# Chapter Seventeen

## ANNIE

"...and so the phone rang again, and the girl answered, yelling, 'Please, I beg of you, stop calling!'" Nancy lifted her head from the giant, ragged book she held open in her lap, her desolate gaze scanning all of our rapt faces. "And the man said, 'You still haven't checked the children. You need to check the children!'"

Gwen clutched my arm, her nails digging into my skin. I had to give it to Nancy, she was really into her storytelling, and she was super creepy. She wore a long-sleeved black dress that covered her from neck to toe, and she wore a wig, the hair long, straight, and black as night.

"I've heard this one before," Bobbee said, leaning over me to whisper at both Gwen and me. "So she's going to call the cops and they say—"

"Ssh!" Gwen pressed her finger to her lips, glaring at Bobbee. "Don't spoil it!"

I bent my head, trying to contain my laughter. I mean

yeah, these stories were scary and Nancy was delivering them in an extra spooky way, but I'd heard most of them already. When I was younger I'd devour those stories and freak myself out. Then watch scary movies and freak myself out even more.

Lifting my head, I glanced around. I didn't see too much kissing going on. Everyone was fully invested in Nancy's storytelling, which was awesome.

I still hadn't found Jake. Where had he gone? Why wasn't he around? He was supposed to be in charge of maintaining the bonfire, but I only saw Brian standing near it, with Hannah by his side, of course.

Nancy had already moved on to another story and I hadn't spotted Jake. Giving up, I watched Nancy get into it as she told the infamous story of the couple making out in a car parked in the middle of nowhere when the announcement sounds over the radio that a psycho just escaped the insane asylum—and he was easily identifiable, since his right hand was a hook.

I'd heard this one before, too. Nancy had a theme going on here—most of her stories had to do with teenage characters—specifically boyfriend/girlfriend types. Love was in the air everywhere, and I was feeling sort of left out.

Pushing my negative thoughts away, I focused fully on Nancy's story, getting into it. She paused and looked around every few minutes, to make sure we were paying attention as the story crept closer to the terrifying ending. I pressed my lips together, noting that everyone sitting around me was deathly quiet, their bodies bent forward as if they were hanging on Nancy's every word, and I found myself doing the same thing.

"...and when the girlfriend got out of the car, she slammed the door hard, a terrifying scream coming from her just afterward. The boyfriend put the car in park and climbed out of the driver's seat, running around to the other side to see what was making his girlfriend scream and cry so hard."

A pause. A beat. A collective sucked-in breath.

"There. Hanging from the passenger-side door handle, was…a…HOOK!"

A hand clamped down on my shoulder the exact moment Nancy yelled the last word, and I screamed. Screamed so loud that I made Bobbee and Gwen and Hailey all scream, too.

Everyone else started to laugh, and I clamped my hand over my mouth, whirling around to see who just scared the crap out of me.

Jake sat there, a sheepish grin on his face, though his eyes sparkled with amusement. "Sorry," he murmured, barely able to contain his laughter.

I dropped my hand. "You scared me to death!" I said with a gasp, shaking my head. I tried to act mad, but it was too hard. I was so happy to see him. So happy that he was sitting behind me, alone, his big hand still on my shoulder. He gave it a squeeze before he removed it, and I faced forward once more, trying my best to act like his touch, his nearness, didn't affect me.

But everything within me trembled in anticipation. What would happen next?

"Yeah. I saw that." A rumble of laughter escaped him.

Jerk. But at least he was a cute jerk.

"Settle down, settle down," Nancy said, and everyone quieted. "Okay, who's ready for another story?"

Jake leaned in close, his mouth near my ear. "Want to get out of here?"

I turned to look at him, our faces close. So close I could see the faint stubble that ran along his square jaw, and I wanted to reach out and touch it.

But I didn't.

"I thought you had to watch the fire or whatever."

"Brian's covering for me." He smiled, revealing straight, white teeth. I wondered if he had worn braces. I wondered what he might've looked like with braces.

Clearly my thoughts were veering way off track.

"Where did you want to go?"

"I don't care." He reached out and brushed a strand of hair away from my forehead, his fingers lightly touching my skin. My stomach dipped and turned. "Just say yes, Annie."

I glanced over at Gwen, who was grinning at me. "Go," she whispered, giving me a nudge.

Ducking, I slipped out of my row and went to the very last row of seats, where Jake was already waiting for me. He stood close, and I tilted my head back to look into his eyes. He was so tall I barely reached his shoulder. "Can we maybe stay here until the last story? I'm kind of having fun."

"Yeah, if that's what you want. I'm down." He shrugged and settled onto the bench, grabbing my hand and pulling me down along with him. We sat so close our thighs brushed against each other, and he slipped his arm around the back of my seat. I rested my hands in my lap, wanting to touch him, too scared to touch him. I'd never been in this sort of situation before, and I didn't know what to do.

Nancy started in on a new story, but I didn't even hear her. My head buzzed at Jake's nearness, my entire body tense. His leg kept bumping into mine as he sat in that way boys do, legs spread as if they wanted to take up the entire world. Usually it annoyed me, but with Jake, I didn't mind. I liked how close he was, how his arm seemed to scoot closer and closer, until finally it was wrapped around my shoulders and he was gently tugging on the ends of my hair, curling it around his fingers over and over again.

I wanted to melt. I sort of wanted to die. But then that would mean I'd never get to experience this again, and I had a feeling that this could be the start of something truly amazing.

Nancy made a gasping, strangled noise, and I jumped, startled. I could literally feel Jake's laughter rumble in his chest and I sort of wanted to smack him. But instead, I leaned my head on his broad shoulder and closed my eyes, breathing deep his clean, soapy scent.

His arm tightened around my shoulders and I kept my eyes closed, savoring this moment.

I never wanted it to end.

· · ·

## JAKE

The second Nancy was done with her storytelling, I was on my feet, Annie's hand in mine as I dragged her out of there.

"Where are we going?" she called after me as we made our escape.

I really didn't know, but I told her, "You'll see," hoping that she'd trust me.

Thankfully, she didn't protest. She just followed behind me until we gained some much-needed distance and I could slow down. Then we walked side by side, her hand still in mine, the both of us quiet as we headed farther away from everyone else.

"Want to go to the beach?" I asked her.

She glanced up at me, her nose wrinkling. "Won't other people be there?"

"Probably." I glanced around and spotted a few couples already camped out near the shore. Guess we all had the same idea. "How about the lifeguard tower?"

"Seriously?" She sounded surprised at my suggestion.

"Yeah. We could see the whole lake from up there. And the stars." It was actually an excellent location. We'd be high above everyone else but no one would really notice us. And I needed to keep this on the down low so my uncle wouldn't catch us together.

"All right," she agreed softly.

We went around the other side of the lake, where the tower was, and once we got there, I encouraged her to climb up first. "For safety reasons," I told her. "I'll be here to catch you in case you fall."

Really I just wanted to check out her ass.

She scrambled up the slats, her butt looking pretty damn perfect in the denim cutoff shorts she wore, and I followed after her, settling in the chair beside her, my arm around the back of it. She scooted close, though she really didn't touch me, and I knew I'd probably have to take this slow. She seemed pretty inexperienced, and I couldn't push her too hard, but man.

I wanted to.

"It's so pretty tonight," she said, leaning forward to peer over the edge of the tower before she lifted her face to the sky. "Remember the last time I climbed up here to join you?"

"When you almost blew my eardrums out with the whistle?" I laughed and so did she. "Oh yeah, I remember."

"I was so mad that you'd fallen asleep and so irritated with you just…in general. It felt really good to wake you up like that," she admitted, glancing over at me.

"Yeah, well, I thought it sucked. Though I also noticed that day you were really pretty." Her eyes went wide and I smiled. "You're especially pretty when you're mad."

She laughed again, though the sound was nervous. "I don't know if you really want me mad at you all the time."

"I don't," I said, reaching out to touch her. I couldn't help it. Her hair was soft and the moon shone down upon it, making the blond turn silvery in color. I tucked a thick strand behind her ear, tracing the curve before my hand fell away. "I like you much better like this."

"Like what?" she asked in the barest whisper.

"You seem…I don't know. Happy. Relaxed." Our gazes locked, and I started to lean toward her, but she averted her head before I could actually kiss her. I slumped back against the seat, discouraged.

"Presley told us she asked you to sit with her tonight," she said conversationally, like it was no big deal she just dropped that bomb in my lap.

I sat up straight. "I tried to let her down easy. I didn't want to make her mad, but I didn't want to say yes, either."

"You don't have to defend yourself. I know she said that just to bother me." She glanced over her shoulder at me, looking so pretty she made my entire body ache with the need to touch her. "Besides, Kyle asked me to sit with him and I said no. Then he said he'd ask Presley instead, since he hadn't kissed her since they were eleven."

Her teasing smile was a distraction until what she said finally sank into my Annie-fogged brain. "Wait a minute. Kyle asked you to sit with him?"

"Well, yeah. I thought you assumed that." When I sent her a blank look she continued. "You were glaring at us in the dining hall earlier."

"Oh. Yeah." I'd been overcome with jealousy and ready to tear him limb from limb.

"I didn't want to sit with Kyle," she admitted softly.

"No?" I was so glad to hear her say that.

She shook her head. "I don't really like him anymore."

"I'm glad." I started to lean in toward her, but Annie turned away from me.

"I never did tell you my secret," she murmured, her head tilted back. "About what happened to me when I was four."

Ah, shit. I didn't want tonight to take a dark turn. "You don't have to if you don't want to," I started, but she shook her head, took a deep breath, and I shut up.

"I want to tell you," she stated firmly. "I trust you."

Those three words warmed my chest, and I waited for her to continue.

"I was four and at a pool party with my parents and my… my baby brother." Her voice faltered, and I frowned. She'd never mentioned a little brother before. "I don't remember much about it, just little bits and pieces in my memory, but I've heard the story many times before, so that's what I'm telling you."

"Okay," I said.

"Anyway, everyone was outside. It was hot and the party centered by the pool at first, but when the sun went down, the temperature dropped. They all moved away from the pool and over to a giant deck that overlooked the city. The house was in the country, on a hill, and it was big. Sprawling everywhere, with gardens and a hot tub and the pool." She kept her gaze firmly on the sky, as if she were telling the stars her story. "I remember my brother kept running away from me. He was barely two, maybe not even two yet. I went chasing after him and we ran around the pool again and again. I remember he kept laughing and so did I. But then he fell in the pool and I—I jumped in to grab him. I don't know how long we were in there together but we were both pulled out about the same time and I survived. He didn't." She turned to face me, tears shining in her eyes. "His name was Rory."

Ah, shit. I didn't know what to say, what to do. "Come here," I told her, opening my arms to her, and she fell into me, her body pressed close to mine, her face nestled in my neck. "I hate that you went through that experience, but I'm glad you survived." I didn't want to tell her I was sorry. I'd heard enough of those two words to last a lifetime and it never felt adequate, especially when it came to my mom.

So I just held her as she trembled in my arms, her breath warm on the sensitive skin of my neck, her hair in my face. I ran my fingers through the silky soft strands until she lifted her head away from my neck, her face so close to mine I could feel her breath feather across my lips. "It's not something I talk about a lot," she confessed softly.

"I can understand why."

"I felt guilty for a long time. Like, why did I survive but he didn't."

"Do you still feel that way now?"

She slowly shook her head. "No. I wouldn't want him to feel guilty if he was the one who lived and I died."

"Is it wrong for me to admit I'm really glad you're alive?" My gaze roved over her face, not sure where I should look—in her pretty dark blue eyes or at her sexy, full mouth? I wanted to kiss her so badly I could practically taste her.

"It's not wrong. I'm glad you feel that way. I'm glad I'm alive, too. I feel lucky." She dipped her head, looking down as she spoke. "I realized last year that if I was the one who died, I'd want him to live life to the fullest. Which was something I really wasn't doing. Until I came here."

"Summer camp changed your life?" I smiled, my fingers sliding out of her hair to actually skim her cheek, tipping her face up so her gaze met mine once more. Her skin was soft, and she trembled beneath my touch.

"No. You did," she whispered, her gaze meeting mine.

# Chapter Eighteen

## Annie

Regret slammed into me hard when I saw his face after I said those words. I wanted to snatch them back, or hit the rewind button and pretend they never existed. He looked shocked, like I'd just stunned him silent with my admission.

I probably shouldn't have said that. I probably shouldn't have turned the night so serious with my confession about my baby brother, either, but I wanted to be open with him. I wanted him to know all of my secrets. And I'd never told anyone what happened to my brother. We moved soon after, my parents wishing for a fresh start. Considering I wasn't in school yet, it was the ideal time to take that chance. Once we moved, no one talked about Rory.

It was like he never even existed.

"You've changed my life, too," Jake whispered and I blinked up at him, seeing the sincerity glowing in his eyes. He licked his lips, his gaze dropping to my mouth, and I knew. I just knew that the moment I'd been waiting for was now.

He moved closer, angled his head as I lifted mine, and my eyes fell shut just as his mouth landed on mine. His lips were soft and full, warm and damp, and they lingered before he slowly pulled away.

My eyes cracked open to find him right there, watching me, so close and all mine to touch. I reached up and traced my fingers along the line of his jaw, the faint stubble growing there abrading my fingertips, and then his mouth was on mine once more. This kiss was longer, deeper. Leaving me breathless, making me want more. His hand cupped my face, his thumb skimming my jaw as I slipped my hand around his nape, diving my fingers into his hair.

His other arm slid around my waist and he gathered me close, his kiss growing firmer, his lips more insistent and making my head spin. A rush of heat swept through my body, and I forgot all about my troubles, my worries, everything, until all I could see and feel and taste was him.

He parted my lips with his tongue, and I let him. He cupped the back of my head, holding me captive, and I let him do that, too. I didn't want him to ever stop. My first kiss was everything I wished it could be, with a boy who meant so much, even though I'd known him for only a short time. But he'd already become more than I could ever truly express to him.

Did he feel the same way? If I could 100 percent trust the way he kissed me, I would say yes. But I didn't know. I didn't think it was all one-sided, our feelings for each other, but I didn't want to be the one who wanted more while he felt differently...

"If I don't stop now, I don't think I'll ever want to stop," he said once we ended the kiss. He pressed his forehead to mine, our accelerated breaths mingled together, and I smiled, wishing he would just kiss me again. I didn't want to talk. We could just express all of our pent-up feelings with our lips attached.

Instead, he pulled away, shifting his arm so it was around my shoulders once more, and we both leaned back against the chair, staring up at the sky. The stars were out in force, since there was only a quarter of the moon making an appearance, and I tried my best to catch my breath. Calm my racing heart, my racing thoughts.

Did I kiss him okay, or maybe it wasn't good enough? I'd never kissed a boy before, and I just followed his lead. But what if he thought I was totally inept? What if he preferred a girl with more experience, one who knew what she wanted and had no fear of going after it? I so wasn't that girl. I was slowly learning how to be brave, but I wouldn't call myself fearless.

All the questions piled up, one after another, especially since he remained so quiet. I started nibbling on my thumbnail, an old habit I'd been trying to break for the longest time.

"Thank you for telling me," he finally said, his deep voice quiet. Steady.

Calming me enough that I dropped my hand into my lap.

"Telling you what?" I kept my gaze locked on the sky, and I could feel him turn to look at me. I liked the way I felt when he watched me. Like I was special. Like I meant something to him.

"About what happened to you, and how you lost your brother." He reached over with his free hand and grasped hold of mine, interlocking our fingers. "We have something in common."

My earlier worried thoughts evaporated in an instant, what with the way he kept sliding our fingers together. He rubbed his thumb across mine, back and forth, back and forth, his touch downright hypnotic, and my whole body tingled when he drew circles on my palm with his thumb. "What do you mean?"

"We both lost someone. Your brother died, and my mom died." He hesitated. "I've never known anyone my age who'd lost someone from their family before. We probably understand each other better than anyone else."

I finally turned to look at him and caught the sadness in his eyes. He held my hand tight, as if he needed the connection, and I angled my body more fully toward him, reaching out to touch his face. He lifted his gaze to mine, the sadness still there, raw and unmasked. He was hiding nothing from me, and I couldn't help but feel honored he believed me worthy enough that he was able to reveal his true self, without all the walls he usually threw up.

"I hardly remember my brother, but you spent fourteen years with your mother." I let my hand drop away from his face, a little embarrassed that I could touch him so easily. This all felt so new, almost surreal. I'd wanted a summer boyfriend, and now I thought I had one, but that didn't mean I knew how to act around him. "That's a big difference."

"Losing them made an impact on our lives," he said. "That you can't deny."

I couldn't. He was right. Because of those we lost, I became the girl who was afraid to live and he became the boy who was angry at the world.

"So maybe finding each other will make a bigger impact on us?" I asked hopefully. "A better impact?"

"I'd like to think that's true, yeah," he said as he leaned in and kissed me again. And again. "You're so beautiful," he whispered against my lips, and because I'm me, I blushed. His fingers brushed my cheeks, the featherlight touch making me shiver. "You're blushing. Your cheeks are hot."

"It isn't every day a boy tells me I'm beautiful," I admitted, a sigh escaping me when he pressed his mouth to mine yet again. I could get used to this. Being held in Jake's arms, his sweet yet hot kisses that made me want more.

"I should make that my new goal. Tell Annie every day just how beautiful she is," he murmured against my mouth. "Because you are. Both inside and out."

That was the nicest thing anyone had ever said to me. And I never wanted to forget it. I never wanted to forget this entire moment.

Long minutes later, we reluctantly agreed that we should head back. He climbed down the tower first, and I followed after him, noticing that he was totally checking out my butt, the perv. He just gave me a big smile when I caught him and smoothed his hand over my backside once I landed on the ground, pushing me against the tower where he proceeded to kiss me until I couldn't breathe.

"Jake." I curled my fingers into the thin fabric of his shirt, feeling the heat from his firm body just beneath. "I need to get back to my cabin."

"One more kiss," he whispered just before his tongue swept inside my mouth. I wound my arms around his neck as he pressed closer, my body trapped between his and the tower. If he kept this up I'd give him one hundred more kisses. I never wanted to stop.

This all felt too good to be true.

• • •

## JAKE

It was too good to be true.

Yet it was true, Annie and I. We were a thing; we were a couple. A couple who had to spend all of their time together on the down low, but yeah. We were together.

And I'd never been so happy.

My good mood spread like a disease. Everyone made note of it, telling me how cheerful I was. Dane said I seemed to have knocked that chip off my shoulder. Brian was glad

I wasn't grumpy so much. Even Uncle Bob told me one morning as I entered the dining hall that he was happy to see my smiling face.

I didn't have the heart to tell him what was causing me to smile. He'd send me home the minute he found out I was with Annie.

So I had to keep her a secret.

She was game for keeping us on the down low. We spent those first heady days we were officially together constantly sneaking around. Sneaking glances. Sneaking touches. Sneaking kisses. It was exciting. Made our mini reunions that much more special, that much more thrilling. She'd smile at me from across the dining hall during breakfast, and I'd immediately break out into a sweat. She'd brush past me when the entire camp got together for the nightly activities, and I wanted to grab her.

And when I'd pull her behind a building and kiss her until she was breathless, she'd stumble away from me, her hair a mess from my hands, her face flushed and lips swollen from our kisses and wearing a blissed-out smile. I'd think every single time, *there goes my girl.*

It was crazy.

It was awesome.

We met for a couple of swim lessons after dark, but those were pointless. No learning how to swim involved. More like splashing each other, grabbing each other, kissing each other.

We couldn't keep our hands off each other. And I needed to slow down. She admitted she'd never had a boyfriend before. That our first kiss on the lifeguard tower was her actual first kiss. She was completely inexperienced. I didn't want to push too hard, but I wanted her so damn bad, it was difficult not to just lunge for her and show her how I really felt.

And right now, I was feeling a lot. So many overwhelming emotions I wasn't sure what to do next. I was just winging this entire relationship and having fun.

But the fun was going to be put on hold when I saw Annie approaching the lifeguard tower, her determined steps and the stubborn set of her jaw making all the hairs on my body stand on end.

I was in trouble. I could feel it.

"Can I come up there?" she asked, shading her eyes with her hand as she looked up at me.

Glancing around, I saw there was no one paying us any attention, so I nodded.

She climbed up the slats and settled on the bench right next to me. I leaned in to kiss her, but she placed a hand on my chest, stopping me. "We need to talk."

Shit. The dreaded *we need to talk* talk. "What's up?"

Annie looked away, the wind blowing hair across her face, and I wanted to reach out and brush it away. But I didn't. "I'm tired of us always sneaking around. It makes me feel like you're embarrassed about the two of us together or something."

"Aw, Annie, do you really believe that?"

She looked at me, pain etched across her features, her eyes full of sadness. Full of doubt. "Yes. No. I don't know. I thought I could handle this, but maybe I can't."

Her words made me tense up. "You knew this was part of the deal. We aren't supposed to be together."

"The summer's almost over. Who cares if we're together?"

"My uncle will care." My dad. I couldn't disappoint either of them. I didn't want to. I wanted to have the best of both worlds, but I hated that I was making Annie feel bad. Worse, that she was mad and hurt over all of this.

"Maybe we could talk to him," she suggested, her tone hopeful. "Maybe we could explain and he'd understand."

"He'd never understand," I said with a firm shake of my head.

Her face fell and she sighed. "This isn't the way I imagined my summer would end up."

"Ah, come on. Don't you like sneaking around?" I lowered my voice, leaning in close, trying to get a kiss, but she wasn't having it. She pressed her hand against my shoulder and gave me a firm shove.

I got the hint. Leaning back, I took a deep breath, giving her distance.

"I did at first," she admitted. "But now…I just want to be normal. I want to walk around and hold your hand. Let people know that you're mine and I'm yours. Don't you want to tell people that, too? Even your uncle?"

Damn, this girl. She was making my heart hurt. "It's complicated, you know this." I wanted to say more. So much more, but my voice abandoned me.

*You're the best thing that's ever happened to me. I'm falling in love with you.*

I couldn't work up the nerve to say it.

"You could sit with me tonight. It's movie night," she suggested.

God, I hated denying her anything. "It's not that easy."

"Why not?" The words exploded out of her. "I've been really patient, Jake. When you wouldn't be seen with me during movie night last week, I was fine with it. When you want to be with me only after dark or making out behind buildings, whatever. I was fine with that, too. But it's getting really old really fast. And you're starting to make me feel bad. Like I'm not worthy of being seen in public with you."

"I definitely don't feel that way about you. You know this," I said, interrupting her so I could get my point across. "It's just that…" My voice drifted and I frowned.

"It's just what?" she urged.

"It's my uncle. It's the entire reason why I'm here. My dad sent me here because we told the judge that I would straighten up and fly right at my uncle's camp. We promised her that I wouldn't break the rules or break the law. I promised my dad that I would listen to my uncle and I wouldn't disappoint them. I'm trying to do right here and not look like a complete fuckup."

Her face crumpled, and she flinched when I dropped the f-bomb. "So being with me would disappoint them? Is that what you're saying?"

"Not at all." I shook my head, my frustration making me snap at her. "Look, I'm sorry. I'm as frustrated as you are about this. But you know it's against the rules for counselors to fraternize with campers."

"So?"

"So I'm a junior counselor and you're a camper."

"We're only a year apart. Isn't that rule in place so I wouldn't, I don't know, hook up with Dane?"

I didn't like hearing her even *say* that. "I guess so. And I really can't stand the thought of you hooking up with Dane."

"That's not the point," she stressed, rolling her eyes. I could tell she was frustrated, too. "I don't want to be your dirty little secret. I like you. You like me. Your uncle seems to like me, too. Why wouldn't he approve of us being together?"

"Because I broke the one rule he stressed to me over and over. He did not want me messing around with campers. He didn't even really want me messing around with other counselors." I glanced down. "And I don't want to disappoint him."

She was quiet for a while, and so was I. I finally lifted my head to check out the lake, then glanced over at Annie.

And she didn't look pleased.

"So we're just messing around, then. I'm like your—fling with Lacey, just longer this time around. Is that what you're saying?"

I hated that she even brought up Lacey. That felt like

forever ago. "No, Annie. That's not what I'm saying." I buried my head in my hands, tugging on my hair so it hurt. "You don't get it."

"No, I really don't get it. And I don't think you get me, either." She stood and went over to the ledge, turning around so she could climb down the tower.

I stood as well, watching her leave. "What are you doing?"

"I'm leaving. It hurts, that you don't want to tell your uncle, or anyone else for that matter, that we're together. I know there are rules in place and you're risking everything by spending time with me, but I just—" She hesitated for the moment, her gaze turbulent. "I just wish we could be together. For real."

Her words practically broke my heart. "I know, Annie. Shit, just…be patient with me, okay? I'll talk to my uncle, I swear."

"You promise?" She dropped to the ground and stared up at me, her expression hopeful.

"I promise," I said solemnly, though there were no guarantees my uncle would approve.

And that was my biggest fear.

# Chapter Nineteen

"He's a jerk," Caitie said.

"Totally," Kaycee added.

"You should dump him," Presley suggested, crossing her arms in front of her chest. "That would show him."

"Aw, I think maybe you should give him some more time? From everything you tell us, Annie, I think Jake's really into you." This was from Hailey, the hopeful romantic of the group.

"Please." Bobbee rolled her eyes. She was our realist. "Keep making him suffer. Or realize that this is just a summer fling and enjoy it while it lasts. Either way, don't give him all the power."

"Why don't you go talk to Fozzie?" Gwen suggested, the ever-so-logical one. The much-needed one in this cabin of crazy. "Tell him that you have real feelings for his nephew, and that you think Jake has feelings for you, too."

Okay, that wasn't a bad idea.

Gwen plopped down on the bed beside me and slung her

arm around my shoulders. Everyone knew I was miserable after my talk with Jake. I was sitting on Kelsey's bunk since she wasn't around. I rarely saw her lately, and none of us had any idea what she was up to. She'd become the mystery girl. Everyone had all sorts of theories except for me.

I'd been too busy enjoying my many secret rendezvous with Jake—until they weren't fun anymore and I started to get a complex.

"Do you really think Fozzie Bear would listen to me?" I asked Gwen.

She shrugged one shoulder. "I don't see why not. He seems reasonable."

"Unless he has that stupid megaphone in his hand. If he starts talking to you with that thing, you're done for," Caitie pointed out.

Everyone in the cabin started to giggle. Even me, and I so needed to lighten my mood right now.

"Let's go sit outside and talk more about this," Kaycee suggested, fanning herself. "It's way too stuffy in here."

It had become unbearably hot these last few days, and I wondered if that was affecting my mood. I guess I could blame it on the heat, though the one who really deserved the blame was Jake.

I knew he didn't want his uncle to find out we were together, and I knew his reasoning behind it, too, but that didn't mean I had to like it. I felt like he could never take our relationship seriously, if he couldn't admit to anyone that we were together. And that hurt. Everything else about our relationship was perfect. Laughing with him, telling each other stories, comparing our likes and dislikes. Kissing him.

Lots and lots of kissing…

He was always so patient with me. And so sweet. I was the totally inept, inexperienced girlfriend and he never complained. Ever. He could. He probably should.

But he never did.

I was the one who finally had to put my foot down first. I was the one who asked questions and pushed him and put conditions on our relationship. And that probably wasn't fair. Who was I to ask him to do all of this for me, when he had so much on the line at home?

Maybe I was the one who was in the wrong.

I followed everyone out onto the front porch, dumping a pile of wet towels onto the ground so I could sit in one of the chairs. The thin cushion was damp from the towels and I winced, feeling the water seep into my shorts.

It sucked. Pretty much like everything else in my life at the moment.

"Hannah is gonna get on us for not cleaning up after ourselves," Hailey said.

We all glanced around the cluttered front porch. There were swimsuits and towels everywhere. Garbage. Flip-flops scattered all over the floor. I was pretty sure I saw a lacy black bra lying discarded under the chair Presley sat in and a pile of candy wrappers under Caitie's chair.

Whoops. Those candy wrappers belonged to me.

"We'll do it later," Presley said with a little groan. "It's too hot to move."

"What am I going to do about Jake, you guys?" I nibbled on my thumbnail, bringing back that old bad habit with a vengeance. I was at a complete loss. I needed serious advice. "I'm so confused."

"You already know how I feel," Bobbee said, and Caitie and Presley nodded their agreement.

It was easy for Presley to agree. She had Kyle now. They were the most popular couple in camp. Not that I was jealous of her relationship with Kyle. I just wished I could walk around with my boyfriend without fear of him getting in trouble.

"I don't know if I want to break up with him. I really like

him," I said miserably. "But I think we're at a standstill."

"You don't want to sneak around, and he's afraid to tell his uncle," Gwen said. "I guess you have a choice. You can either talk to his uncle, or you can continue to sneak around and always feel like he's hiding you for another reason. Eventually you'll become paranoid, get angry, and then in a fit of rage, you'll end it for good."

I blinked at her. "Sounds like you have it all planned out."

"No, I'm just observing your situation from the outside. I can see exactly that happening, though. Who wants to be treated like they're a secret? It's fun at first, but after a while, you start developing a complex," Gwen explained.

"That's exactly it!" I practically started bouncing in my chair. Gwen understood me so well. "I'm more than halfway to the complex right now."

"Right, it's understandable, your feelings. So. Can you stand the idea of being apart from him?" Gwen asked.

Tears threatened at ending it with him. I just…I couldn't even fathom it. "No," I admitted.

"Then talk to Fozzie. Plead your case."

"Should I do that now?" It was a Sunday, the last full Sunday we'd be at camp, which meant lots of free time and rare sightings of Fozzie Bear, since he spent most Sundays in his office.

"It's the perfect time," Hailey said with an encouraging smile. "Go fight for love, Annie."

I stood, faltering at the idea of *love*. It was such a serious word, with so much meaning behind it—a life-altering, potentially devastating meaning. Could I be in love with Jake? We'd only known each other for such a short time. Yes, I liked him a lot. I cared about him even. I could see myself falling in love with him, but was I at that point now?

I really had no idea.

Determination filling me, I stood, slipped on my flip-flops, and took off, with everyone from the cabin cheering behind me. I headed along the trail, my gaze drawn to the lake and the lifeguard tower on the other side.

I could see Jake sitting on top, his baseball cap on backward like usual. No shirt, just those red board shorts, and I could make out the width of his shoulders even from where I stood.

Strong shoulders I'd leaned on. Shoulders I'd even dared to kiss. I'd come to depend on those shoulders, on that boy. That I was willing to fight for him by talking to his uncle surely proved that, right?

But the closer I got to the main building—and Fozzie Bear's office—the more nervous I felt. What if he wouldn't listen to me? What if my admission got Jake in trouble? That was the last thing I wanted to do.

Yet I couldn't let this end without a fight, either.

I entered the building, nearly sagging with relief when I felt the cool, air-conditioned breeze wash over me. Fozzie's secretary lifted her head from the magazine she'd been looking at, a welcoming smile on her face.

"Can I help you?" she asked. I was fairly certain she never took a day off. Like, ever.

"Um, can I talk to, uh, Mr. Fazio, please?" It took everything inside me to keep from blurting "Fozzie Bear."

She held up her index finger and picked up the phone, hitting a button while she waited for him to answer. "A camper is here to speak with you. Annie McFarland." A pause. "Yes, I'll send her in." She hung up and our gazes met. "Go ahead. Just knock on his door before you enter."

*Or what? Will I see something I could never unsee?* Nerves eating at my stomach, I smiled at her. "Thank you."

I walked down the short hall, coming to a stop in front of the partially closed door with the sign ROBERT FAZIO on the front of it. Curling my hand into a fist, I tentatively knocked, and Fozzie's booming voice ordered me to come in.

I don't know why the man bothered with that megaphone. He was pretty loud without it.

"Annie McFarland. To what do I owe the pleasure of your visit today?" He smiled at me, and I had to remind myself that he was a human being, just like me. I couldn't be scared.

"Um, I'd like to talk to you." How did his secretary remember my name? There were hundreds of kids here, so I was impressed. And a little scared. Maybe there was a reason they knew who I was.

And it had everything to do with Jake.

He waved a hand at the empty chair sitting opposite his desk. "Sit. Relax. Enjoy the air-conditioning." He grinned.

My nervousness wouldn't allow me to smile, so I practically fell into the chair, curling my hand into a fist so I wouldn't start chewing on my thumbnail again. I needed to act like I had it together. But it was so hard.

Fozzie leaned forward, peering at me. "What did you want to talk to me about?"

"Jake."

His extra-thick eyebrows rose. He looked almost comical, not that I could laugh. "What about Jake?"

"I know he's your nephew," I started, and Fozzie nodded.

"I think everyone knows he's my nephew."

"Well...I, uh, really like him."

Those bushy eyebrows lowered.

"And he really likes me. A lot."

The eyebrows were now scrunched because he was frowning.

My palms started to sweat. "We, uh, we've been sort of seeing each other for the last few weeks, and I really care about him. Jake cares about me, too, and we—"

"What?" The one word blasted out of him like a bullet. All glimpses of sweet, lovable Fozzie Bear the camp director were gone. He looked positively furious. "How old are you, young lady?"

I was completely shocked by his tone. "Um, sixteen."

"There will be no fraternization between campers and counselors!" He picked up the phone receiver and stabbed a button, shouting when his secretary answered, "Find Jake now!"

My heart felt like it just fell into my toes.

· · ·

## JAKE

It was so damn hot out, I felt like I was sweating out every single drop I drank. There weren't even many kids in the water, the sun and the heat were so intense. Couple that with the humidity and it was like no one even wanted to move.

Including me.

I'd found one of those spray bottles with a fan attached a few days ago in Uncle Bob's office so I was spritzing myself constantly. Thank God for the umbrella shade that kept me mostly covered. I'd melt away if I didn't have that thing.

Not only did the heat make me miserable, but also my recent conversation with Annie left me down, too. I didn't know what to do about her—more like, I didn't know what to do about Uncle Bob. If he hadn't laid down the law so firmly, I'd be strutting around this place with my arm around Annie. I wouldn't care who knew we were together.

We only had a few days left, and then camp was done for the summer. I probably shouldn't care if he caught us together. But I didn't want to disappoint him. I didn't want to upset my dad, either, because even if Uncle Bob found out this last week, I'd bet money he'd ship me back home. Or call my dad and demand he come pick me up.

I didn't want to deal. I didn't want them mad at me. For

once, I wanted to prove to them I was a good guy. That I could clean up my act and do the right thing. I didn't want this summer to be wasted.

But to not acknowledge that Annie and I were together would be a wasted summer, too. If she could just be patient, we could declare to anyone and everyone that we were a couple once camp was finished. Then it wouldn't matter anymore.

Right now, though, it still mattered. A lot.

I glanced to my left to see someone running toward the lake. Squinting, I brought up my binoculars to see it was my uncle's secretary.

My stomach churned and I dropped my binoculars. This didn't look good.

"Jake!" she screamed once she got close enough. "Your uncle needs to talk to you. It's urgent!"

The churning turned into full-blown nausea. "Is everything okay?" What if something was wrong with my dad?

She waved an impatient hand. "Hurry!"

"What about the tower?"

"I already told Dane. He'll cover for you. Come on!"

I scrambled down the tower and chased after her, passing her with ease and I was only jogging. My heart raced triple time as I contemplated the many reasons why Uncle Bob would need to see me so urgently.

And it all came to a skidding stop when I entered his office to see Annie sitting in one of the chairs, softly crying.

She glanced up at me, tears streaming down her cheeks as she kept whispering, "I'm sorry," over and over again.

Turning my head, I saw Uncle Bob sitting behind his desk, his beefy arms crossed in front of his beefy—fine, pudgy— stomach. "You have something to say for yourself?"

I felt like I was eight and had just got caught busting out that dining hall window with a baseball—true story. I had to work kitchen duty for a week when I was here that one glorious summer. I hadn't minded a bit.

This was much worse.

"I don't know what you're talking about," I said, refusing to let myself look at Annie. All I really wanted to do was go to her and wrap her up in a hug. I hated to see her cry.

"Well, your father is on his way. I'm sure you can explain it to him then."

"You called my dad? Why?" It felt like my heart was in my throat. I could hear Annie behind me, the soft crying, the sniffles. The anger that blazed in Uncle Bob's eyes, his gaze going to the side as his mouth drew into a thin line. It dawned on me that he was gesturing toward Annie, and I knew right then what happened.

He knew. He knew about the two of us.

But how?

"It's not what you think—" I started to say, but he shook his head, cutting me off with a look.

"It's exactly what I think, because Annie told me everything." He dropped his arms and they landed on the edge of his desk. "Why, Jake? I told you that was the one rule you couldn't break, and you did it anyway? I thought you were better than that."

"It's not what you think because this is more than me breaking your rule," I explained, needing him to actually listen to me for once. "Annie is more than just a—"

"She's more than what? Another one of your conquests? I wouldn't be so sure about that. You don't think I don't know what goes on around here? I have eyes, son. I know about you and Lacey."

Shock rendered me speechless.

"And I know you ended it with her before you two got out of control. Trust me, she came right to me and ratted you out," Uncle Bob said. "But when I realized you weren't spending any, ahem, quality time with her, I let it go. You seemed to be on the right track. Now there's this." He shook his head, his disappointment with me radiating from him in big, giant waves.

I felt like one of those waves just plowed into me and stole my breath.

Whirling around, I stared at Annie's bent head, anger making me want to lash out. I pressed my lips together, exhaled shakily, and just let it all out. "You actually told him?"

She lifted her tearstained face, our gazes meeting. Her eyes were filled with even more tears, and I refused to let them hurt my heart. I was too pissed to want to offer comfort. "I thought I could convince him that what we had was real. That we both wanted it."

"Yeah, well, thanks for convincing him to kick me out of here." My words made her flinch. "Is this what you really wanted? Are you getting back at me because I made you sneak around, so you decided to make me disappear instead? Well, congratulations, it worked."

"Annie, it's probably best if you left now," Uncle Bob said, his voice soft. "Grab some tissues on the way out, okay, honey? You have snot running down your face."

She leaped to her feet, let out a frustrated little growl, and walked out of the room.

Effectively walking right out of my life.

I almost shouted "don't go," but what was done was done. She probably didn't mean for me to get kicked out of camp, but she should've come to me first. This was my life she was fucking with.

She did a damn good job of it, too.

"Is my father really on his way here?" I asked, my voice raspy. I felt like I was going to cry now. And I hadn't done that since Mom died.

Uncle Bob nodded. "I didn't tell him what you did wrong. I thought I'd leave that explanation up to you."

Great. My dad wouldn't listen to me. I knew he wouldn't. He'd think I screwed up, and he'd want to get me out of here as soon as possible. He'd probably hardly give me a chance to pack up my stuff. Now I'd miss out on the last week of camp, miss out on saying good-bye to my friends, to Annie.

Though she'd given me the worst kind of good-bye that any girl ever could.

"Go pack your things. " And with that, I was dismissed. Not allowed to plead my case. Not permitted to even beg for my job back.

I would've, too. These last couple of weeks, I'd grown closer to people. I had friends. I taught the little kids how to swim. I led my first paper-airplane craft class and had half the seats filled. I'd made an ass of myself in a skit with Dane a few nights ago, and everyone had laughed. I'd dressed up as a mummy during a ghost-telling round and scared the hell out of the little kids.

I also had a girlfriend. A girl who understood me, who held me close, whose smile lit me up inside and whose laughter made me feel whole. When she kissed me, touched me, looked at me, I felt like I could do no wrong.

But I could. I was fallible. I was weak. Annie was my one true weakness.

Somehow, she'd used it against me.

# Chapter Twenty

## Jake

A knock sounded on my cabin door before it creaked open and I heard footsteps. I kept my back to the open door, my duffel sitting on my bed as I continued to stuff my clothes inside. I didn't even bother folding stuff. I didn't care. I just wanted out of here before everyone saw me being escorted out by my father and uncle like I was some sort of criminal.

I almost wanted to laugh. Technically I *was* a criminal. I wouldn't be surprised if my dad brought handcuffs and put them on me before shoving me in the backseat of his car. He'd drive me straight to the courthouse, where that judge would pound her gavel and send me to juvenile hall. Or worse — jail. I was seventeen, after all. Pretty damn close to being a legal adult.

"Jake." Dad's familiar voice said my name. "Son, turn around and look at me."

I stopped what I was doing and tilted my head back, staring up at the wooden slats of the ceiling. I didn't want to turn around. I didn't want to face his wrath. Bad enough how angry my uncle got at me in his office and in front of Annie. Talk about humiliating.

"Jake. Come on."

I frowned. He didn't sound mad. But he was real good at masking his feelings.

Slowly, before he started yelling, I turned around.

My dad stood in the open doorway, wearing a T-shirt and black cargo shorts, his sunglasses were on his head much like mine are most of the time. He looked tan, fit. More than that, he looked…happy?

My frown grew in intensity. Was he happy that I'd failed yet again? No freaking way.

"Your uncle is being ridiculous." Dad entered the room and sat on the edge of my bed. "You should unpack your stuff. You're not going anywhere."

"What?" I asked incredulously. I felt like I was being jerked around. *Leave! Stay! Pack! Unpack!*

"You're not leaving. I convinced your uncle that you didn't break some cardinal sin." I gaped at him and he shrugged. "So you have a girlfriend who's a camper. So what? I did the same thing with your mother, and look at how good we turned out."

I snapped my mouth shut. "Wait a minute. You told me you and mom met here at camp."

Dad nodded. "We did. When I was a junior counselor and she was a camper, much like you and your girl now. I know I said you should do the right thing the last time we talked, but after our phone conversation, I thought about my time here. When I met your mom and we fell in love."

I remained quiet, watching the many emotions pass over my dad's face, my heart aching thinking of my mom. Of losing her. My heart ached even more at the thought of losing Annie, too.

"I told Bob he was making too big a deal out of it.

Teenagers fall for each other here every summer. You can't fight love." Dad's smile was nostalgic. "I met the love of my life here. Being at camp is bringing back lots of memories. Good ones."

I missed her, too. Life was good when she was alive. My parents rarely fought. They were a solid unit and grossly in love. I only say "grossly" because when I was younger, I couldn't handle seeing them kiss each other all the time, considering I was a typical punk-ass kid. They were so incredibly close, I think that was why my dad was so devastated when she died. He didn't have his partner anymore. He relied on her a lot. And so did I.

"I miss her," I said, my voice scratchy.

Dad met my gaze. He didn't look angry or upset with me, and I couldn't help but feel relieved. "I do too, son. I miss her a lot."

"But you never talk about her."

"It was too hard." He sighed and shook his head. "And that was wrong of me. I've been thinking a lot while you've been gone. I missed you, too, you know."

"You did?" I was surprised.

"Absolutely." He reached out and ruffled my hair, but I ducked away from his hand before he could mess it up too bad. "Can I tell you something?"

"What?"

"Your uncle did the same thing." Dad hesitated. "Dated girls at camp."

"Seriously?" I could hardly wrap my head around it.

He nodded. "He—how do you kids say it today—hooked up with plenty of girls, especially when he became a counselor."

"I find that hard to believe," I muttered.

"It's true. I think it was the megaphone."

I busted out laughing. I couldn't help it. "He had it back

then?"

"He sure as hell did," Dad said, chuckling and shaking his head. "I went and talked to your Annie."

The laughter died. "She's not mine."

"Aw, come on, Jake. You're going to pull that? She only did what she thought was right."

"And what was that? Telling on me? Getting me busted? Because that's exactly what she did." I paused, ran my hands through my hair. "He was so *angry*, Dad. He wouldn't even listen to me. Just told me to pack my stuff and that you'd be here soon."

"He was mad at himself more than anything. That's what he told me, at least. When I sent you here for the summer, I gave him implicit instructions that you weren't allowed to get away with shit." My dad's face became serious. "You had a way of worming yourself out of everything since you were a little kid, and it got worse after your mom died. You became so angry. And then you started acting out when I wasn't paying attention to you, and you were feeling neglected. I didn't see it that way then. Only recently have I been able to figure this all out, you know."

Surprise coursed through me at his admission. "I was angry. And sad."

"I know. I was, too. I just didn't know how to deal with it."

"Me, either," I admitted softly, hanging my head. I blew out a harsh breath. "Do you think she did this on purpose and tried to get rid of me?"

"Absolutely not. She was devastated at the thought of you leaving. Even more devastated that you were mad at her."

"Then how can I fix all of this?"

"Well, first you need to go talk to your uncle. He'll say sorry, you'll say sorry, he'll give you your job back, and you're here for the last week."

"What about me and Annie?" I lifted my head. "I said

some mean things to her, some things I regret, all because I was mad. I don't know if she'll forgive me."

"Do you care about this girl, Jake?"

I nodded, trying to swallow past the choked-up feeling that clogged my throat. "A lot," I croaked.

"Then if she feels the same way about you, I'm sure she'll listen. And I'm sure she'll forgive you." He smiled. "Just brush yourself up on your begging-for-forgiveness skills first. That's my recommendation."

His words made me smile, but I was still a nervous wreck inside. "Thanks for convincing Uncle Bob that I'm not a screwup, Dad."

"He knew you weren't a screwup. He mentioned that you'd been doing a great job around here this summer, especially the last few weeks. Does it have anything to do with you being together with Annie?" Dad raised a brow.

I shook my head. "She's changed me."

"For the better?"

"Yeah." I was embarrassed, admitting this stuff to my dad. "She's made me see I don't need to be so angry all the time."

"You'd better not let go of this girl, Jake. She sounds like a keeper. She reminds me of your mother."

"What?"

"One of those quiet, sweet girls. The kind that makes you realize one day that the perfect girl has been sitting in front of you all along." He smiled, his tone wistful. "If she's anything like that, make it right."

I nodded, my mind spinning with all the possibilities. I needed to make it right with Annie.

But how?

• • •

ANNIE

Would I ever stop crying? No, I didn't think so. Though I needed to get a grip because the tears were blurring my vision and I'd just tripped over a branch in the middle of the trail that I should've noticed, since it was about as big as my leg.

But no, I kept thinking of how angry Jake had looked. How furious the normally sweet Fozzie Bear had been. What a nightmare. I hadn't gone back to the cabin, not wanting to hear any more input from my friends. I knew they meant well, but they'd be so mad at Jake for saying those things. I didn't want to alter their opinion of him and make it even worse.

So I hung out in the arts and crafts building for a while, helping Nancy clean up and organize everything. Keeping busy took my mind off everything for a little while, though I still felt sick to my stomach over what happened and what Fozzie Bear said.

I figured Jake was just lashing out. He thought I told on him to his uncle, so I could understand why he was so upset. That he wouldn't even let me explain why exactly I told Fozzie about us frustrated me to no end, but what else could I do? Fall to my knees and beg Jake to listen to me?

No way.

It had been reassuring to talk to Jake's dad. Fozzie's secretary spotted me crying near the volleyball courts and called me over, escorting me into an empty office where a handsome man who vaguely reminded me of Jake had been waiting. When he introduced himself to me as Jake's dad, my knees had started knocking together. I figured he was going to rip into me just like Jake.

But he didn't. He was so nice, offering me kind words and asking me to be patient with both Fozzie and Jake. He explained what happened, how frustrated he'd been with Jake at the end of the school year. How he shipped Jake off to camp with all of these expectations and rules. And how he fully expected his older brother to keep watch on Jake and not let him get out of line.

"It was all because of me," Jake's dad had explained, his expression earnest, his brown eyes so like Jake's it was uncanny. "I'm the one who didn't want Jake to fail, and my brother took it to heart." He smiled. "Us Fazios are a passionate bunch."

I could only nod in agreement.

"Don't give up on my son. Let him grovel a little bit, of course, but if you can find it in your heart to forgive him, I think he'll do right by you," his dad had said.

I didn't want to give up on Jake, but I did think he needed to definitely grovel. And I needed some time alone. To think. That's why I was hiking one of the trails around the lake. I had a water bottle and wore my thinnest tank top since it was so dang hot. I'd sneaked off, not telling anyone where I was going because I didn't want Hannah to tell me no. I'd wanted to hike in peace.

That's why it was so shocking when I plowed right into someone, nearly falling on my butt I hit them so hard. This was what happened when you walked with your head bent and your thoughts in the dark clouds.

"Annie! Are you all right?"

I glanced up at the familiar voice to find I'd run into two someones. Kelsey and one of the girls from cabin G7B. Sylvia, I think was her name.

And they were holding hands.

When they saw my gaze drop to their linked hands they let go of each other and took a few steps apart, putting distance between them.

"I-I'm fine." I nodded and wiped at my cheeks, hoping I had no stray tears running down my face. I tried to smile and act like I was okay when I so wasn't. "What are you two up to?"

"Oh, nothing." Kelsey sent Sylvia a weird look, one I'm

pretty sure I could decipher since I was proficient in sneaking around.

*Busted.*

"Look, I'm going to head back to the pool. Bye, Annie. Thanks for your help, Kelsey!" Sylvia said cheerfully, waving at us both before she ran down the trail back toward the camp.

Kelsey sighed as she turned to look at me. "You're going to tell the girls, huh?"

"Tell them what?"

"That you caught Sylvia and me holding hands." Kelsey's shoulders sagged. She looked utterly defeated. "Go ahead, tell them all I'm a big scary lesbian and then they'll freak out and never want me around again."

I was sort of shocked that she just called herself a big scary lesbian, but really? That didn't matter to me. I just liked her for her. "That's your story to tell, Kels. Not mine. I can keep a secret. Trust me. Though I don't know why you're hiding it, considering Courtney and Riya were a thing during first session."

Everyone knew about Courtney and Riya, and no one seemed to care. Why should we? They were two nice girls who happened to be in a relationship. I hated that Kelsey felt like she should sneak around.

Kelsey pressed her lips together, looking on the verge of crying. "My parents will freak."

"They don't know?" I asked softly.

She shook her head and sniffed. What was it with today and all the crying? "They sort of know. They think it's a stage. It's why they sent me back to camp. They figured I needed to get away from, and I quote, bad influences."

Huh. Seemed like everyone treated camp as a place to get away from everything else.

"But now I've met Sylvia and…I really like her. She likes me, too. We just don't feel comfortable being together in front of everyone. We don't want them to make fun of us."

"I get it. Well, not fully, but I understand how hard the sneaking around is. How it puts a toll on you and her and your entire relationship." I told her a brief summary of what just went down with Jake and his family and how he nearly got kicked out because of me, and we both ended up in tears. Sitting on a hill, passing my water bottle back and forth and wiping our eyes with the hems of our tank tops, we were a sniveling mess.

"I wish you wouldn't have excluded yourself so much," I told her once we got ourselves together. "The girls really are nice. They're just kinda hard to get to know at first because they're such a tight unit."

"I figured they'd hate me if they knew the truth," she admitted.

"Well, I can't guarantee every single one of them will be comfortable with it right away, but they all say nothing but nice things about you, Kelsey. They like you." I reached out and touched her arm. "I like you, too."

Kelsey stared at the lake. "I'm sorry if I cut you off. I didn't mean to. I just, I didn't know how else to react. I've always had a hard time making friends."

"You didn't act that way on the first day at camp," I reminded her. "I thought you were kind of crazy."

Kelsey grinned. "I pretty much dared myself to approach you. You looked so lost and nervous, exactly how I felt. So I thought we could unite together."

"Well, let's try to stay united for the last week while we're here, okay? I know you want to spend time with Sylvia, but spend time with us at the cabin, too. It'll be fun." I smiled. "I promise."

"What about you and Jake?" she asked.

I glanced down, staring at the ground. "I don't know." I shrugged. "He's probably still mad at me."

"I bet he wants to talk to you. He's not leaving, thanks to his dad. I bet he's looking everywhere for you," Kelsey said.

"You think so?"

"Definitely." Kelsey smiled.

I lifted my head, trying to return the smile, but I couldn't. I should go look for Jake. Tell him I was sorry. Wait for him to tell me he was sorry. Then we could kiss and make up and have the best last week ever.

Could that really happen, though? Or was I being too idealistic?

"I hate that it's the last week." Kelsey's smile faltered. "It went by so fast."

"Too fast. But we need to make the most of it, right?"

That was my plan, at least.

# Chapter Twenty-One

ANNIE

"You have to take this new class with Nancy," Bobbee practically gushed as she guided me into the bathroom. "It's going to be so much fun."

She made me sit on a chair that was brought in from the front porch and I did, glancing around. "Why do I need to take this class? And why did you bring me into the bathroom?"

"Because you love arts and crafts, silly!" Bobbee gave me this face like I was being a total dork. "And I'm going to do your hair." She wrapped her fingers around the band that was holding my floppy topknot in and tugged it right out, taking a few hairs along with it.

"Ouch!" I batted her hand away. "Why are you bothering doing my hair?"

"Have you looked in a mirror lately? Just because you're on the outs with your man doesn't mean you can't clean yourself up a little bit and look decent," Bobbee said.

It was only the next day after the big fallout, and I'd been giving Jake some space, secretly hoping he would come and see me first, but he didn't. I didn't see him in the dining hall this morning during breakfast when I usually did. I hadn't seen him all day, period, and it was already after lunch.

"I don't know if I want to go to the new arts and crafts class," I mumbled, wincing when Bobbee started brushing my hair. The girl showed no mercy.

"You should. Kelsey told me about it. She'll be there."

I liked how Kelsey just inserted herself back into the group. She was making an effort, and I was glad. All of the girls were happy to have her back around.

"If this is Jake's airplane-making class, I'm not going."

"It's not! I swear. It's similar, though. Some sort of origami class."

"Is he teaching it?" Did he have other hidden talents I wasn't aware of?

"No. He hates arts and crafts. He's out at the lake, like usual. Maybe you want to go swimming?" Bobbee's eyes sparkled as she looked at me.

I'd come clean last night about the swimming lessons, about my fears, though I didn't tell them exactly why I was scared or about my little brother. I wasn't ready to share all of that yet, but they totally understood. Plus, they thought it was hot, how I'd dared Jake to give me swimming lessons. *All the touching and naked skin!* they'd all pretty much chorused.

That they could give me grief over the fact that I couldn't swim said a lot about my confidence level. I was over worrying if they thought I was a loser because I didn't like the water that much. I'd gotten better, but I still had a long way to go. "You know I hate the lake." I shivered just thinking of all the critters that lurked in the water.

"I know, I was kidding. But seriously, take this class. I'm doing it, too. It'll be fun."

"Fine," I said with a sigh, feeling melancholy but trying to push past it. This was my last week at camp, after all. I needed to make the most of it.

I let Bobbee do my hair, not wanting anything too over the top, so she just straightened it with her flat iron. Then Gwen came in, a big, fluffy brush in her hand, meaning she wanted to do my makeup. I let her do that, too, thinking they all just wanted to cheer me up.

Once we finally left the cabin, I realized they were acting sort of weird. Like, *giving each other goofy looks and giggling for no reason* weird.

"What's going on?" I asked them.

They all went silent. "Nothing," they chorused.

Uh-huh.

By the time we walked into the arts and crafts building, I saw that the tables were filled with girls. Like, every spot was taken with the exception of a table that sat in the front. There was a tented piece of paper sitting in the middle of the empty table with the word RESERVED written on it in bold black.

"Kaycee made sure that we'd have a table," Hailey reassured me as we went to sit.

Nancy appeared before us a few minutes later, looking frazzled as usual, her hair everywhere and her skirt flowing about her legs as she paced back and forth. "So excited to show you guys how to make these. When I was a kid we called them fortune tellers, though I remember other kids calling them cootie catchers."

We all laughed, as did she. She started passing out sheets of paper to each table and we took a piece, waiting for her to give us instructions.

"Now, when I was in hmm, the sixth grade? My friends and I would make these all the time. And usually we just used lined paper out of our notebooks. The key is that once you get the folds just right, you need to make sure the right things are written inside, you know?"

We nodded, but I could tell most of us didn't know. I had no idea what she was even talking about.

"Here's an example." Once she returned to the front of the room, she held up the oddly folded piece of paper, then slipped her fingers into the bottom, splaying the paper wide one way, then another. "The numbers are chosen at random. So you open it up and choose, let's say, five." She moved the fortune teller with her fingers, counting off four beats. "Then you choose another number, say two." She moved it twice. "Then you lift up the triangle-shaped paper to read your fortune." She did just that and started to laugh. "'You will marry Fozzie Bear.' Heaven forbid."

We all laughed. Then we started folding our pieces of paper as she walked between the tables, giving her usual gentle encouragement like she was so good at doing. She even dropped off example fortune tellers at every table and I picked ours up, examining it.

"You should play with it, Annie," Bobbee encouraged.

"If anyone needs to hear their fortune, it's you," Kaycee said.

Shrugging, I slipped my fingers into it and opened it wide. "I'll choose number four." It was my favorite number. When I opened and closed it four times, I then chose the number five. "This is dumb," I said as my fingers moved the paper back and forth.

"This is all they had to do back in the 80s," Presley said solemnly. "They must've been so incredibly bored."

Kelsey started to laugh, and I smiled, peeling back the fortune behind the number five. My breath lodged in my throat when I saw the words written inside.

*You will kiss Jake Fazio by the end of the day.*

"Okay, whose idea of a joke is this?" I asked, my voice trembling.

Gwen frowned. "What's it say?"

I showed it to her, and her eyebrows shot up. "Do it again."

I did it again, choosing different numbers this time. When I peeled back the paper and read the fortune, I gasped out loud.

*You will fall madly in love with Jake Fazio...or maybe you're already in love with him.*

"Oh God," I whispered, not knowing if I should laugh or cry. I stared at my friends' faces, but none of them looked guilty. They didn't even look too innocent, either, if you know what I mean. "Did one of you make this?"

They all shook their heads.

Blowing out an exasperated breath, I did it yet again and this time my fortune said:

*You will collect your final swimming lesson tonight at eight o'clock.*

"Says who?" I asked aloud, though no one answered me.

"Are you okay?" Gwen asked, nudging me with her elbow.

"I guess." Shrugging, I tore open the last fortune that I hadn't read, not bothering going through the pretense of choosing numbers.

*You will be Jake's date at the talent show on Friday.*

*I will, huh?* "I just wish I knew who made this," I said, my gaze roaming over my friends' faces yet again. But they all ducked their heads, trying to hide their smiles.

An intricately folded paper airplane landed directly in front of me. Written across one wing were the words "I did."

And on the other wing it said, "I'm sorry."

Turning in my seat, I found Jake standing there as if he were waiting for me, a hopeful expression on his face.

I stood and went to him, the fortune teller still in my hand, my legs shaking as I approached. My heart ached at seeing his gorgeous face, how his gaze warmed as he watched me come closer. I stopped just before him and held the paper fortune teller toward him. "You made this?"

He nodded. "Nancy taught me how this morning."

My heart melted. So did the bones that were in my legs. "Why?"

"It's my way of saying I'm sorry. And I messed up. That I hope you can forgive me and we can make the most of this last week we have with each other."

I threw myself at him, not caring if the entire room was watching. I just needed to touch him, to feel his arms come around me. And when they did, when they held me close and squeezed, his mouth at my temple in the softest kiss, I had to close my eyes against the new tidal wave of tears that threatened to fall. "I'm sorry, too," I said as I pulled away so I could look up at him. "I shouldn't have told your uncle — "

"I'm glad you did," he said, cutting me off. "You telling Uncle Bob brought my dad here, and we had a good talk."

I smiled, blinking away the tears. "So did we."

He chuckled. "I know." Reaching out, he wiped away the one tear that streaked down my cheek with his thumb. "Let's spend the rest of the week together, okay? And make the most of it?"

I nodded, and he kissed away another stray tear, his lips lingering on my skin.

The entire room burst into applause and happy laughter, and I tried to untangle myself from his arms but he wouldn't let me. He just held on tighter and bent his head, his mouth at my ear. "Let them look. Let them think they had a hand in pushing us back together, but we know the truth."

I lifted my head, my gaze landing on his lips. "What's the truth?"

"You can't fight fate. We were meant to be, Annie." His head descended, his lips brushing mine as he spoke. "We belong together."

And then he kissed me.

# Epilogue

## ANNIE

My phone rang, and I frowned when I saw Jake's name flash across the screen. "Why are you calling me?" I said in answer.

He chuckled, the sound rich and warm and making me wish we were in the same room together instead of hundreds of miles apart. "Nice to hear your voice, too," he said teasingly.

"I thought we were going to FaceTime each other." I sounded sort of bratty, but I really liked seeing his face every day, and I was missing him extra hard. This long-distance relationship thing was difficult, yet we somehow made it work. But it was Thanksgiving break and without school filling my days, I was missing Jake even more than usual.

"I'd rather call you." Something rustled, and I heard the faint *tick* of a turn signal in the background. "What are you up to?"

"I was watching a movie." I shut my laptop and set it aside on my bed. I'd stayed locked up in my room mostly for the last three days, and I was already bored out of my mind. I'd never wanted a school break to go by fast as much as this one.

"Anything good?"

"Not really." I could tell he was in his car by all the background noise I could hear. "Are you driving?"

"Maybe."

"You shouldn't be talking on the phone while driving," I reprimanded him. "It's against the law."

Jake laughed. "Thanks for the reminder, good girl." His voice softened. "And don't worry about me. I'm almost where I need to be."

"Where are you going?"

"Hold on." He must've put his hand over the phone because everything became muffled. I waited patiently, wondering what he was doing, why he wouldn't tell me what he was up to. Maybe he had family to visit for the holiday. We were planning to see each other during winter break, and that couldn't come fast enough. "Okay, sorry about that."

"You're being very mysterious." I leaned back against my pillows and stared up at the ceiling. It was cold out, and rainy, the weather fitting my mood. I thought back to warm summer days and spending them with Jake. We hadn't been in each other's presence since the last day of camp, and that had been such a bittersweet moment. One I relived over and over. I remembered the way he held me, the words he'd whispered in my ear, how he kissed me like he never wanted to stop.

"I've missed you," he said, clearly changing the subject.

"I've missed you, too." I lowered my voice, always worried Mom or Dad was lurking outside my closed door. "I wish it was already Christmas so we could really be together."

"What would you do to me if we were together? In the same room? Right now?"

I could feel my cheeks go hot. That he could make me blush while we talked on the phone said a lot, especially about what I wanted to do with him if I ever got him alone.

"Hug you."

"Ah, come on, you can be more creative than that," he teased.

"Kiss you."

"With tongue or without?"

"*Jake.*" My cheeks were blazing hot.

"Let me tell you what I'd do if we were in the same room together." He hesitated for the barest moment, just long enough for me to hold my breath in anticipation. "I'd pull you in for a bone-crushing hug, then I'd push you away from me because I'd want to see your face and look into your eyes."

Everything inside me melted. He was a closet romantic, I swear. "What next?" I whispered.

"Then I'd cup your face and kiss you. For a long time. With plenty of tongue."

That sounded positively dreamy.

"Annie! Come downstairs!" Mom suddenly yelled, interrupting my lust-fueled thoughts.

Sighing irritably, I told Jake, "Hold on. My mom wants me."

"Don't hang up," he said as I rolled off my bed and went to the door.

"I won't," I promised as I started down the stairs. Mom stood in the living room, a strange smile curling her lips. "What's up?" I asked her.

"Someone's at the door for you." She waved at the still-closed front door before she went into the kitchen.

Frowning, I looked from the door to her retreating back to the door once again. "Why isn't it open?"

"Open the door, Annie," Jake gently encouraged.

Oh. My. God.

My heart started to race and I ran for the front door, throwing it open to find Jake standing on my front porch, his phone still clutched to his ear, a giant smile curving his perfectly kissable lips.

"You're here," I said breathlessly into the phone, at him. *Him.* He stood directly in front of me, wearing a black sweatshirt with the hood pulled over his head, his eyes taking me in, raking over me from head to toe. I rested a hand on my head, feeling the messy bun there, and I grimaced, ending the call between us with a press of my finger. I shoved the phone into my sweatshirt front pocket as I walked out onto the porch. "And I look terrible."

He pocketed his phone as well and took a step closer. "Stop. You look beautiful. Shut the door, Annie."

I did as he asked just before I was pulled into his open arms. We held each other close, my cheek pressed against his damp sweatshirt. His heart thumped wildly beneath my ear, and I breathed deep his citrusy scent. I couldn't believe he was here, with me. Wrapped all around me like he never wanted to let go. "Why are you here?"

Jake stepped away and his hands went to my face, cradling my cheeks. "I convinced your parents to let me see you during Thanksgiving break."

My lips fell open. "How?"

He took his advantage and kissed me, his mouth warm and soft, connecting with mine again and again. Until I parted my lips and his tongue slid against mine in the deepest, most bone-melting kiss I've ever experienced in my life.

"Haven't you figured out I'll do just about anything to be with you?" He finally said long, kissed-filled minutes later. His lips moved against mine when he spoke, and I smiled, unable to contain my happiness that he was actually here. In my arms, his mouth on mine, our gazes locked.

This was my biggest dream come true.

"I'm so glad you're here," I murmured before kissing him again. His hands dropped from my face to grip my hips, pulling me in, his persuasive mouth on mine pulling me under...

A very familiar someone cleared their throat and I leaped away from Jake, my gaze going to my mother standing in the open front doorway. "Hi, Jake," she said, her tone faintly amused.

"Hi, Mrs. McFarland." He slipped his arm around my shoulders and tugged me in close to his side. "Thank you again for helping me with my surprise."

"You're welcome." Her expression shifted into serious mom mode. "You two behave yourselves, okay? Remember what I told you, Jake." She sent him a meaningful look before she stepped inside and quietly shut the door.

I turned to look at him. "What did she tell you?"

He smiled and wrapped his arms around me, his gaze never leaving mine. "She told me I had to respect the rules of their house." We both laughed at that. We always had to deal with the rules—and how to work around them. "No sneaking around. No closed doors. You know, parent stuff."

"Parent stuff," I repeated amusedly. I stood on tiptoe and kissed his jaw. "So you're going to be on your best behavior while you're with me?"

"Oh, yeah." He kissed the tip of my nose. My cheek. My lips. "But what they don't know won't hurt them, right?"

"Are you saying you want to sneak off?" My brows shot up.

"I can't lie that I'm hoping for some alone time with you." His fingers drifted across my cheek, making me tremble. "Maybe I should dare you to break your parents' rules. Though I know you're not much of a rule breaker …"

The rain had stopped, the clouds breaking apart to let a beam of sunlight in. Just like my mood had lightened, the weather had, too. I swear my heart threatened to burst out of my chest, I was so happy.

"I'd break the rules for you," I told him, my eyes falling shut when his mouth hovered above mine. "I have before."

"I know," he murmured against my lips. "My beautiful good girl."

"My wicked bad boy," I whispered back, the both of us laughing softly.

Until our laughter slowly dissolved into nothing but sweet, hot kisses.

# About the Author

*New York Times*, *USA Today*, and number one international best-selling author Monica Murphy is a native Californian who lives in the foothills below Yosemite with her husband and children. A workaholic who loves her job, when she's not busy writing, she also loves to read and travel with her family. She writes new adult and young adult romance and is a firm believer in happily ever after. She also writes contemporary romance as *USA Today* best-selling author Karen Erickson. Visit her online at www.monicamurphyauthor.com.

*Discover more Entangled Teen books...*

## The Boyfriend Bet
### a *Boyfriend Chronicles* novel by Chris Cannon

Zoe Cain knows that Grant Evertide, her brother's number-one nemesis, is way out of her league. So naturally, she kisses him. She's thrilled when they start dating, non-exclusively, but Zoe's brother claims Grant is trying to make her his "Ringer," an oh-so-charming tradition where a popular guy dates a non-popular girl until he hooks up with her, then dumps her. Zoe threatens to neuter Grant with hedge clippers if he's lying, but Grant swears he isn't trying to trick her. Still, that doesn't mean Grant is the commitment type—even if winning a bet is on the line.

## Resisting the Rebel
### a novel by Lisa Brown Roberts

When loner Caleb Torrs sees spirit committee leader Mandy Pennington pining over some los-er at a party, he thinks she's lost her mind. Maybe he has, too, because he just asked her to be his fake girlfriend. She'll get that guy's attention, and he'll get his stalker ex off his back. Too bad their plan is working, and the loser she wanted is finally noticing the one girl Caleb just might be falling for...